HANGMAN'S REACH

When Crado Bluestone buys some cattle to start his own ranch, it comes as a brutal shock when he is accused of being a rustler and is strung up from a tree. The real cattle thieves, led by a killer named Monk Purvis, leave him for dead. Help is close at hand, however, in the form of a Texas Ranger, who rescues the hapless cowboy just before he chokes to death at the end of the rope. But revenge burns deep in Bluestone's heart to even the score . . .

DALE GRAHAM

HANGMAN'S REACH

Complete and Unabridged

LINFORD
Leicester

First published in Great Britain in 2016 by
Robert Hale
an imprint of The Crowood Press
Wiltshire

First Linford Edition
published 2019
by arrangement with
The Crowood Press
Wiltshire

A catalogue record for this book is available
from the British Library.

ISBN 978–1–4448–3978–4

Published by
F. A. Thorpe (Publishing)
Anstey, Leicestershire

Set by Words & Graphics Ltd.
Anstey, Leicestershire
Printed and bound in Great Britain by
T. J. International Ltd., Padstow, Cornwall

This book is printed on acid-free paper

1

Black Mesa

The tall stranger paused on the edge of town. A lazy hand rested easily on the pearl-handled .44 Colt Frontier strapped to his hip. A double-action Smith & Wesson Schofield was tucked into a cross-draw holster: a solid back-up if needed. There he waited, searching for the unusual: anything that didn't quite fit the expected pattern. Eagle-sharp eyes scanned the down-at-heel berg. It was a well-honed procedure refined over more years than he cared to recall.

Always check out a new place. Give it the once-over. Such a rough appraisal had saved his bacon on more than one occasion. His brisk nod confirmed that all appeared as it should. No surprise packages filled with hot lead.

The old wound in his left shoulder from a stray slug still gave him jip. That unwelcome legacy had been acquired when he was greener than a newborn calf: a mere fledgling in his profession.

Its acquisition had been a near-death experience that had rudely taught him one vital lesson. Man-hunting was most definitely no easy-going pastime for the fainthearted. The accuracy of a man's shooting prowess was just as important as a fast draw. In fact, the two skills went hand in glove and required constant practice if an edge was to be maintained.

But it was total detachment under fire, a calm unruffled determination, that mattered most. Nerves of steel were the key element that separated survivors and their victims. Anything less and you were a dead man. After recovering from the injury Crado had tracked the other guy for two months. The knucklehead had not understood that vital maxim and was now residing on boot hill in Dodge City, Kansas.

Satisfied by what he saw, a light nudge had the black Arab stallion moving off down the middle of the street. Single-storey adobe structures of Mexican origin soon gave way to more recent erections of clapboard. Some of these, wishing to affect a more permanent appearance, had adopted false fronts with ornately carved overhangs. Paint, however, was in short supply. Those premises that had been given a splash of colour soon found it peeling away under the harsh Arizona sun.

Black Mesa was just another cluster of shanties stuck in the middle of nowhere. Perhaps it owed its existence to being on the northern edge of Arizona's notorious Sonora Desert. This vast expanse of sand and rock was the last obstacle for travellers aiming to cross the border into Mexico.

As such it attracted a host of n'er-do-wells and riffraff seeking to evade the long arm of the law. Gunslingers rubbed shoulders with gold prospectors. The newcomer gave a satisfied nod of approval. Yes indeed, there was plenty of money in a place like this, as the numerous saloons and dance halls testified.

The lack of a law office appeared to prove the assumption, although a sign advertising the presence of Judge Roy Benedict holding court on behalf of the vigilance committee each Wednesday afternoon testified to some semblance of order. How much authority the said official carried in such a town was still open to question.

Adjacent to the legal representation pinned to a notice board was a Wanted poster, which was of far more interest to Crado. It appeared to show there was more adherence to the law in this berg than he had so far assumed.

He drew the black cayuse over to the office and stepped down. It was a slow, sinuous movement, more akin to that of a snake than a man. A deliberate action that once again afforded time to survey his surroundings. Those who perused such hoardings usually had more than a

4

passing curiosity in mind.

A mean-eyed unshaven desperado with a twisted expression stared back at the assessor. Crado could almost smell the disdain oozing off the penned depiction. Judging from past experience, such drawings were usually quite accurate. Expert pensmiths were able to capture the essential qualities of felons from descriptions offered by surviving witnesses.

The wanted man on this poster was a pox-scarred greaser going under the whimsical cognomen of El Vengador. Accused of robbery and murder, no further details of the *bandido* were given. Not that Crado was bothered. It was the cool $1,000 reward that piqued his interest. *Dead or Alive* brooked no dispute. Clearly The Avenger had upset people in the locality who were now demanding retribution.

Crado Bluestone was the man to answer their need.

He was about to tear the poster down when a high-pitched voice broke in on his pondering. The interjection sounded more like the squawking of a strangled chicken than any human speaker. Crado stifled a chuckle.

'You interested in taking on the job, stranger?' enquired a stout red-faced dude rather lacking in height. His thumbs were hooked into the pockets of a silk vest with the intention of making the guy look important. 'Step inside my office and I can fill you in on the details. Judge Royston Benedict at your service.'

He was well-dressed in a blue serge suit and clearly enjoyed his food. The buttons on the vest, complemented with gold watch and chain, were straining at the leash. The grey stovepipe was intended to increase his diminutive stature. An expectation that failed miserably, merely giving the critter a somewhat comical persona.

Credo briefly surveyed the legal adjudicator from head to foot.

'No need, Judge,' he drawled, sticking a cheroot into his mouth. 'Unless of course you know where I can find this bad boy?' His raised eyebrows hinted that he suspected a positive response would not be forthcoming.

'All I know is that he tried to seize the monthly gold shipment bound for the smelter at Prescott. It was a miserable failure. But during the scuffle one of the guards was wounded and the other one killed — he was the only son of the mine owner,' the little man hurried to add, hoping to kindle the guy's interest. 'That's why the company has offered such a good reward for his capture. But I've had word from the nearest official law office in Tucson that he's wanted for a heap more crimes.'

Crado shrugged. 'All very interesting, Judge, but no darned use to me. I need to know which way he took off if'n I'm gonna bring him in . . . or otherwise, depending on his attitude.' He struck a match on the wall and lit up. Blue smoke dribbled from between clenched teeth. 'If'n you can't fill me in, guess someone over yonder can provide the answer.'

He nodded towards the welcoming doors of the Del Rio saloon. Then, without uttering another word, he ripped down the poster and strode across the street.

The judge was left impotent and spluttering. But in a place like Black Mesa he chose not to voice his disapproval aloud. That guy looked like he knew how to handle the pair of hoglegs straddling his lean hips. So he settled for an aloof sniff before waddling back inside his office.

Four other horses lined the hitching rail fronting the saloon. Their heads drooped as they patiently awaited the return of their owners. As a matter of routine Crado checked the saddles. Yet another habit he had cultivated since that dire episode five years previously. None of the saddles elicited any reaction other than a shrug.

He lifted his head towards the heavens. Somewhere in this vast wilderness was a saddle that had once belonged to him. When he finally managed to track down the new owner, his days as a man-hunter would be over. As would the thief's allotted spell on this Earth.

Crado paused under the veranda of the saloon. His leathery features hardened.

The gleam in the ice-blue eyes overflowed with vindictive retribution. There was a reckoning to be had. It was now long overdue. Gnarled fingers traced the ugly scarring around his neck. Time had tempered the savage injury. But it still felt like a rough scarf. His face creased up into a twist of revulsion.

Yes indeed, there was a price to pay, and Crado Bluestone would exact the full measure when the time came. As sure as egg is eggs, it most assuredly would. That was a promise he had long since made to himself.

Thoughts of terminal justice flicked his mind back to that day on the Brazos. Those five long years now seemed like a lifetime away. Yet the scene was still clear as a bell, as if the events had happened only the day before.

2

Left Hanging Around

The first day of May 1871 shone bright and cloudless. A warm sun on the lone cowpuncher's back had lulled him into an easy-going detachment. He was feeling on top of the world. Life was good, and it was going to get a whole lot better.

He was driving a bunch of thirty steers to the piece of land he had recently bought with a loan from the Texas Land Agency in Sweetwater. Not much of a herd as yet, it was nevertheless a start. From small acorns do big oak trees grow. The cowboy had ambitions to build his holding up to be the largest in West Texas.

Unlike his more boisterous sidekicks, Crado Bluestone had saved almost every dollar of his meagre pay earned by punching cows. It had taken many years of frugality working on a host of different spreads throughout the Lone Star State.

In his pocket he now had the means to turn his dreams into a reality. The steers had been bought from Harvey Stride who owned the Broken Wheel ranch at the head of the valley. Once he had bedded them down, all he had to do then was head for town and make the first down payment. Then it would be full steam ahead.

A smile crossed the cowpoke's craggy face. Life was indeed good. A herd and a ranch house, even if the house was only a soddy at the moment. Next he would need to find a wife with whom to share his dream. And there was none fairer than Lilly May Kendrick, who ran the candy store in Sweetwater.

The idyllic aura surrounding the seasoned hand was suddenly shattered by a harsh command to hold up.

'What you doing with those steers, mister?' demanded a heavyweight jasper holding a Remington Rider in his huge mitt. The star pinned to his vest indicated he was a Texas Ranger. 'They're sporting the Broken Wheel brand on their hides. My reckoning is that you've stolen them.'

The man pressed forward as he pushed out the accusation. He was a good fifteen years older than the three deputies who accompanied him. They quickly spread out to block in the accused rustler. All had their guns drawn.

'Mr Stride don't take kindly to skunks that rustle his beef,' piped up a scrawny wisp of a runt calling himself the Pecos Kid. Young he might be, but Crado couldn't help noticing that his gun hand was rock steady.

Stunned by the blunt accusation, he quickly recovered.

'I bought these steers fair and square.' Vehemently he protested his innocence. He reached into the pocket of his hide jacket. 'Here,' he said, holding up a piece of paper. 'This is a bill of sale signed by the boss man himself.'

'Let me see that,' snapped the ranger. He gave it no more than a brisk once-over before striking a match and setting it afire. 'Don't look much like a bill of sale to me, eh boys?' A raucous bout of chortling accompanied the flaming invoice as it fluttered in the dry air.

'Hey, you can't do that!' objected the startled cowpoke. This sudden change in fortunes had taken him completely by surprise.

'I just did,' guffawed the leader of the posse, adding with forceful menace. 'Now shuck that gunbelt. You're under arrest.'

'You've gotten this all wrong,' Crado hollered out. Panic gripped his innards at the turn that this ugly situation had taken. 'Take me to see Stride and he'll confirm the sale. The Broken Wheel ain't far from here, just down the valley apiece.'

'We ain't got time for that, fella,'

growled the older of two brothers who had pushed forward. Whiff Rankin was a lean rake of man. Downwind it was easy to see how he had acquired his handle. An unlit cigar was stuck between his broken teeth. 'Do like the ranger says, or get blasted out the saddle.'

Not wishing to be outdone by his domineering elder sibling, Lije Rankin butted in:

'We don't need to waste the time of the courts to administer justice round here, do we, Monk?' The query was addressed to the leader in a heavy lisp as Lije removed a lariat from the saddle horn. 'This varmint is guilty as hell. There's only one way to deal with skunks like him.'

To the unknowing, the youngster's voice invited ridicule. At least five rash greenhorns were now interred with their boots on, due to having tried to make fun of the youth with their mocking prattle.

'Guess you're right at that, Lije,'

concurred the leader.

Before Crado could make any further protest a well-tossed lariat encircled his body. Whiff quickly picked up on his brother's deftly performed action and followed suit. The cowboy's arms were now effectively trapped. Much as he struggled to free himself, he was securely pinioned.

'This ain't justice,' the unfortunate victim remonstrated. A fiery surge of anger had invaded his whole being as the truth dawned. 'And you buzzards ain't real lawmen at all. I'm figuring that you're the rustlers here, not me.'

'Enough of this jawing,' rasped the gang leader, who was fast tiring of the charade. All the same, he was still determined to act the part of an avenging vigilante lawman. 'Get him over to that cottonwood. We'll show this scumbag what we do to thieves caught on the Brazos.'

'Sure thing, Monk,' concurred Lije Rankin. He and Whiff quickly dragged Crado's horse over to the lone tree.

A rope with a ready-made noose on the end was thrown over an overhanging branch. The Pecos Kid stuck it over Crado's head and tightened the thick knot. Noticing the bulge in Credo's jacket, he extracted a billfold stuffed full of banknotes.

'Hey, lookee here, boys!' he exclaimed, holding up the find. 'We sure struck lucky today. Not so good for you though, mister.' His ugly smirk lacked any hint of levity.

'Reckon I'll have that fine saddle when we're done here,' said Monk. 'Mine's all but finished.'

The innocent cowpoke was totally impotent, unable to move or prevent the theft both of his cattle and of the future life he had planned. Too late he regretted not accepting Harvey Stride's offer of help to move the herd. Now his life was about to be snuffed out, forfeited, and there was nothing he could do about it.

One minute he'd been rejoicing in his good fortune, the next he was facing extinction. In the flick of a rattler's tongue it would be all over.

Pecos looked to Monk for the final curtain call. The gang boss raised his hat, revealing the natural tonsure that had given him the nickname. A brisk nod and a slap on the animal's rump followed. The horse bounded forward, leaving the victim helpless and choking. What an awful way to die, gasping out one's life on the end of a rope. Both Crado's legs pedalled frantically, trying to relieve the choking pressure on his neck. It was a reflex action that only served to tighten the noose.

'Yeehaaah!' hollered a gleeful Lije Rankin. 'Don't he just kick, boys?'

Crado's eyes bulged wide. His breathing, laboured and rasping, soon became ever more faint as he struggled to draw in what little air was still available. The excruciating torment was no quick-fix way to shed this mortal coil. It could easily last for twenty minutes or more. The days of fast exits on a trap door had not yet reached many law enforcement agencies in the wild territories of the West.

A woodpecker perched on the branch above the victim's head. Its chirruping song was strangely melodic amidst the onset of death. Then it flew away, unmindful of the gruesome termination being enacted below.

But it was the insane chortling at his predicament by the killers that would be the last human sound the victim heard before oblivion overcame him.

Eager to be away from the scene of their hideous crime, Monk Purvis and his three sidekicks herded the steers off towards the Crosby Heights, where the current base of their operations was hidden away amidst the remote labyrinth of arroyos.

Meanwhile, Crado's desperate yet futile efforts to free himself were becoming weaker by the second. Ten anguished minutes had passed. The end was surely fast approaching. All those dreams were now nothing more than an incoherent blend of flashing images.

Then it happened. A shot rang out cutting through the hideous torment. Suddenly he hit the ground. The slackening of the pressure around his throat brought instant relief. Yet all he could do was lie where he had fallen, struggling to drag air into his tortured lungs.

He must have passed out. But for how long? The next thing he knew, a man was dribbling water down his torn throat. It felt like pure nectar.

'Don't speak until you're ready.'

The words sounded far away, in another world. More water helped to revive him. Five minutes passed before he could sit up. His saviour was sitting on a log smoking.

'You ready to spill yet, mister?' A languid nod of Crado's head brought the good samaritan forward. 'So what happened here?'

To begin with the victim's garbled response emerged as little more than a choking whisper. The stranger dumped his smoke and moved in closer to hear the gravelly-voiced account. It took some considerable time, and numerous pauses to draw breath, for the sorry episode to be recounted.

'The name is Jack Banner,' the man replied when Crado had finished. 'I'm a Texas Ranger sent from Fort Worth to investigate all the rustling that's been taking place on the Brazos of late.' He held up a scrap of charred paper. 'This is all that's left of your bill of sale. I was sent here because one of our men was killed last month. He must have been getting too close to the truth and was gunned down by these jaspers. Any ideas as to their identity?'

'One of them called the leader Monk,' Crado mumbled.

'Monk Purvis!' exclaimed the Ranger, suddenly animated. 'He's the rat I'm after. The varmint must have read about how the Rangers were sending a man to hunt down these rustlers. It was in all the papers. He killed my partner Ezra Quinn and must have stolen his badge. These fellas sure are playing a vicious game.'

Crado nodded. 'I noticed a copy of the *Amarillo Sentinel* poking out of his jacket.' Attempting to stand, he rasped out, 'I need to get after them, Mr Banner. They can't have gone far.' He tottered no more than a step before falling over. His legs felt like jelly and a fit of nausea caused him to retch violently. More water helped settle his stomach. Although by then much improved — how could he have been any worse? — the cowboy was still extremely weak and debilitated.

'You're going nowhere without a horse,' countered Banner, firmly but gently pushing him down. 'As it is we'll have to ride double to the nearest town. You need a doctor to dress that neck. Looks like a lump of raw steak from where I'm standing.'

The survivor knew that Banner was right. Every move he made was excruciating, especially where his shirt rubbed on the badly lacerated neck wound. It was a slow ride to the nearest settlement of Amarillo.

★　★　★

Over the coming weeks, Crado slowly recovered his strength, The thick welt encircling his neck settled down. It no longer caused him pain. But according to the sawbones he would carry the ugly scar for life.

With all his dreams shattered, Crado could think only of revenge. Catching up with Monk Purvis and his buddies to exact a full and terminal reckoning was at the forefront of his thoughts. He declared his intentions to the Ranger.

Jack Banner was less than enthusiastic. Primarily a solid lawman, he deplored any kind of vigilante reprisal. Playing the card proposed by Crado was not an option as far as Banner was concerned. He impressed this view vehemently upon the angry cowboy.

'Let the law take its course,' he

advised the seething man firmly. 'Else you could end up in the same jailhouse as those skunks.'

But Crado was adamant that he was going after the critters no matter what. During his period of recovery he had been asking around.

'According to my information, they've left Texas and have headed west into New Mexico territory, where you have no jurisdiction.'

Banner could only shrug his shoulders. His hands were tied if that was the case. As a Texas Ranger, his bailiwick ended at the border.

'Looks like I'm hogtied,' he declared acidly. 'But there is one thing I can do.' Crado eyed the Ranger askance as he went on to explain: 'I could make you a temporary US marshal. That will give you the authority to bring these varmints in. Go it alone and you'll find yourself in no-man's-land. Dead or Alive, my way puts the law on your side. So what d'you say?'

The Ranger's proposition sounded

like the best option for him to pursue his quarry.

'Reckon it's a deal, Jack,' he said.

Banner made him swear an oath of allegiance to uphold the law of the United States before handing over the much-coveted official badge of office.

'It will be valid wherever you travel and you will have the full backing of the law,' the Ranger told him, but a warning accompanied the solemn moment. 'It only holds good provided you obey the code of behaviour expected from the proud office you now hold. Abuse it for your own ends and I'll forget about borders and come a-hunting you down myself.'

Crado promised to adhere to the creed. He was touched by the Ranger's faith in him. Nobody had ever before trusted him to that extent. His lower lip trembled. With a curt nod he acknowledged the confidence placed in him and his understanding of the conduct expected of him. The two men shook hands.

Credo left Amarillo on a fine black stallion provided at the expense of the Texas Rangers. He named it Dusky. Over the next few weeks, he tracked the gang across the plains of the Texas panhandle into New Mexico.

3

Man-Hunter

At about the same time as Crado was being sworn in as a US marshal Monk Purvis had decided it would be opportune for the gang to split up until the heat died down. In his warped mind the killing of a Texas Ranger was far more serious than that of some hick cowpuncher. The Rangers might not have jurisdiction outside the state, but that didn't stop the word being put about. He breathed a sigh of relief when the New Mexico signpost had been passed.

The current batch of stolen cattle now numbered well over a hundred. Knowing they were safe from pursuit by the Texas Rangers, Monk took time out to rebrand the stolen beeves and sell them on to the army. Good quality beef was a welcome change from buffalo meat. A price was agreed with no questions asked as to the beef's origins.

Monk and the Pecos Kid then headed west for Arizona. With money burning holes in their pockets, the Rankin brothers wanted some fun. They clearly assumed that by hopping over the border into New Mexico they were safe from any kind of pursuit.

It was a bad decision that was to cost them dear.

★　★　★

Crado arrived in the border town of Clovis on a Sunday morning. A bell was tolling in the tower of the church at the far end of the main street. Apart from the odd few worshippers, nobody else was abroad. Most were likely sleeping off the previous night's excesses.

His first port of call was the sheriff's office to register his presence and ask about any strangers in town. Deputy

Ike Toomin stretched his bulky frame as the newcomer entered. He had been asleep at his desk. On being questioned about the gang of rustlers, his shoulders shrugged to indicate ignorance.

'I only got back last night from chasing up a stage robbery on the Hobbs road.' His voice was slurred, the watery eyes half-closed. 'Best place to ask after any strangers is over at the saloon. Baldy Portalis is the man to see. He knows about every coming and going here in Clovis.' The lawman's rheumy gaze had lifted on spotting the much respected badge of a US marshal. 'Guess you must be chasing up some heavyweight dudes, Marshal?'

'Much obliged, Deputy,' said Crado, ignoring the lawman's curiosity. 'So where's the real sheriff hang out? Perhaps I could ask him?'

Toomin huffed. 'A place the size of Clovis only merits a deputy,' he grumbled. 'Those tight-fisted jaspers at head office always claim hard times when I ask for a raise.' He slung a thumb towards the door, clearly piqued at the newcomer's gibe. 'Saloon's across the street.'

Then he tipped his hat down and slung his feet back up on to the scarred desk beside a half-empty bottle of whiskey. That was clearly all the guy had to offer.

Crado spat on to the dirt floor and left. So much for any official help. He ambled across to the Blue Dahlia. Once inside the drinking den he looked around the dim interior. The familiar odour of stale beer, sour sweat and burnt fat never failed to make his nose wrinkle. There was no need to look for Portalis. The light from a smoky tallow lamp cast its lurid yellow gleam on the bartender's shiny pate.

Surprisingly, the saloon was quite busy. Maybe at weekends it never closed. The newcomer sidled over to the bar and ordered a beer.

'Deputy Toomin reckons you can help me,' he said, addressing the lugubrious egghead.

Portalis grunted with frustration. 'That guy should be paying me for all the information I dish out,' he complained in a woebegone sigh of acceptance. 'Lazy good-for-nothing. So what is it you want to know, stranger?' Then his eye lit upon the badge of office. Instantly the barkeep's attitude changed. 'G-guess it must be impportant for a US marshal to be asking?' he stammered.

'You could say,' drawled Crado, sipping his beer. 'I'm tracking four owl hooters who could have passed through here.' He went on to describe Monk Purvis and the Pecos Kid.

Portalis perked up quickly, interrupting: 'Sure I remember them two jaspers. They had plenty of dough to toss around. Good tippers as well. But they pulled out over a couple of weeks back. Reckoned to be headed for Arizona.'

Crado cursed his bad luck. 'What about the other two,' he shot back. 'They're brothers. One's a scrawny beanpole, the other a young punk with a lisp.'

Portalis stiffened. The blood drained from his ruddy features. Crado instantly picked up on the barman's unease. His icy gaze froze the man to the spot. 'You seen these dudes recently?' he pressed, in little more than a sibilant murmur.

The barman's nerve-shredded gaze slowly lifted to the tobacco-stained ceiling.

'R-room number f-five,' he burbled. 'You're talking about the Rankin brothers, Whiff and Lije. They'll be sleeping off last night's carousal with two of my gals. There won't be any shooting, will there, Marshal? Those are my best chicks up there and they ain't easy to replace.'

This plaintive query received a brisk shrug of indifference. 'All depends if'n them dudes decide to cut up rough, don't it?' The implication was clear.

Crado checked his guns, the Colt Frontier and the Smith & Wesson Schofield that he had taken to wearing in a cross-draw holster. The extra gun was another suggestion from Jack Banner. Satisfied, he then moved across to the stairs leading to the upper storey.

Silence descended as the general hum of conversation faded away. A tense atmosphere took hold of the clientele, who watched open-mouthed as the marshal slowly mounted the stairs. The threadbare carpet was just sufficient to muffle his approach along the corridor.

Number Five was at the far end. Even through the closed door the rumble of snoring was clearly audible.

Time for a wake-up call.

Standing to one side, he drew his Colt and rapped three times on the door. A series of muffled grunts was followed by some female squawks. But there was no further response to the summons. Crado gave another three raps. This time the groaning was louder and hinted at an irked reaction to the unwelcome disturbance.

'Who's there?' croaked a slurred

voiced befuggled by sleep.

Crado's mouth twisted in a warped grimace. There was no mistaking the lisp of Lije Rankin. Crado made no reply other than to hammer on the door again.

'Get lost, knucklehead!' This time it was the voice of the repugnant Whiff Rankin. 'You're disturbing us.'

Having secured their attention, the visitor announced his business.

'Sorry to disturb you, gentlemen,' he declared in an official voice. 'But I have an important letter here for a Mr W. Rankin. It needs a signature.'

That announcement certainly caught their interest. 'Just a minute while I get dressed. Then I'll be with you,' replied Whiff. Then he mumbled under his breath. 'This better be worth getting me out of bed for.'

As soon as he opened the door Crado grabbed him round the neck and hustled him back into the room. His revolver was pointed at the stunned figure of Lije Rankin who was splayed out across a half-naked girl. He was just about to partake of an early morning passion breakfast.

'Party's over, boys. Get your clothes on,' rapped the visitor. 'We have an appointment at the jailhouse.'

Whiff struggled to free himself but the butt end of Crado's gun cracked across his head curtailed any dissent. He fell to the ground, out for the count.

One of the girls screamed, grabbing a blanket to cover her exposed flesh.

'What the heck . . . ?' Lije's outburst ceased as he recognized the figure of the man who, he had assumed, would now be stoking the fiery furnace. Ashen-faced, his mouth dropped open. He burbled out some unintelligible lisped gibberish.

'Reckon you've seen a ghost, Lije?' Credo said with a smirk. He shook his head. 'Na! It's me all right. The poor sucker you robbed and left for dead on the Brazos. But this time I'm gonna make sure it's you pair of buzzards that take the hangman's reach.' His gun hand waved menacingly. 'Now get dressed and lug that piece of dog dirt along with you.'

Turning his attention to the shaking girls he observed, 'Looks like you ladies have earned yourselves a few easy bucks. Now shift those perty asses . . . pronto.' The girls needed no second bidding to stuff the money into their bodices. Then they took a hasty departure.

Crado hustled the two despondent prisoners downstairs. Passing through the main room of the Blue Dahlia, he called out, 'Easy as falling off a log, Baldy. No need for any shooting with lunkheads like these to deal with.'

Deputy Toomin was shaken into wakefulness as Crado took it upon himself to lock up the two woebegone rustlers. Returning to the office, he slapped the Wanted dodger of the Rankin brothers on to the desk. This pair of no-goods were each worth a cool $300. This had been a good day's work that would set him up fine to continue his search for the other two rats.

Unfortunately, being new to the job of law enforcement, even if it was only as a voluntary unpaid officer, he was not privy to the full extent of his rights and responsibilities. Ike Toomin was not slow to fill him in.

'As a badge-carrier you only receive ten per cent of the reward money,' he declared in rather too breezy a manner. 'The rest goes to the county.'

Crado blustered, but he was too stunned to utter any coherent protest. This was definitely not what he had been expecting. Toomin was adamant, and even showed him the decree in a county rulebook. Once he had paid over to Crado his share of the reward money from a safe, the irked bounty hunter left, promising himself that things would change in the future. Clearly, being the proud wearer of a US marshal's badge had its hang-ups. Most conspicuous of which was the disadvantage of it not being such a lucrative calling as he had expected.

A month later he ran across the Pecos Kid while trailing him across a sandy wasteland of which the name translated as the Journey of Death. The *Jornado del Muerto* offered travellers no water and little shade. Initial preparation prior to departure was, therefore, essential if the journey were to be completed unscathed. Pecos had failed to heed the warning before he left Carrizozo.

Crado found the Kid gasping out his last breath beside the fallen carcass of his horse. He offered no resistance when the vigilante arrested him. Water was his only thought. Crado purposely taunted him by slowly consuming a tin of peaches. Each mouthful was savoured to the full. Yet even this torment failed to elicit the information he most desired.

The Kid had no idea as to where Monk was headed. They'd split up in Corona.

A string of lurid curses issued from the captor's throat, as he realized that the trail had gone cold.

'I'll find you one day, Monk,' he railed impotently, shaking a fist at the arid terrain. 'If'n it takes a lifetime, I'll hunt you down.'

Had he known that many years would pass before that day came, perhaps Crado Bluestone would have abandoned his man-hunting quest. But with the benefit of hindsight not an option, he hoped that Purvis might well be run to ground in the next town.

Following his recovery from acute dehydration, Pecos tried to ingratiate himself by handing back the billfold he had stolen. The gesture received short shrift seeing as there was no money left inside. Indeed, Crado was so incensed he took it as an insult. A single blow to the jaw laid the Kid out. Crado followed up with a boot in the Kid's ribs. A sharp crack brought forth a pained yell from the Kid.

'Aaaaaagh! You've done broke my

ribs,' he yelped, clutching his side.

Much as the chastizer would have liked to continue the punishment, he curbed his rising temper. He was no bullying molester and instantly regretted his uncontrolled outburst of anger.

Crado left the Kid to mop the blood from a split lip. He walked away berating himself for losing his cool. But his innate good humour soon reappeared. He felt pleased with himself. Once again, the man-hunter had succeeded in capturing his man without a shot being fired.

The rest of the desert crossing took a further two days of hard travel. Little was said between guardian and prisoner. All of the Pecos Kid's time was spent nursing his aching torso. Indeed he was actually glad when they reached civilization.

The first major town on the far side of *El Jornado del Muerte* was Williamsburg. When Crado presented the Wanted poster along with the sorry specimen it depicted, on this occasion there was no disclosure of his marshal's status. The incumbent law officer accepted the damaged goods without a second glance.

'I'll have the local sawbones look him over sometime today,' Abel Jukes remarked casually, turning the key in the cell door. 'Should be fit enough to stand trial next week when Judge Frizell arrives. Will you be around to give evidence?'

'Only if'n I'm needed,' Crado replied. 'I'm heading further west to try my luck in Arizona.' Before replying, his ardent gaze had settled on a Wanted dodger pinned to the notice board. Monk Purvis was now worth animpressive two grand — Dead or Alive! There was no penned depiction, but that ugly mush would be pasted on to his mind until he had finally erased the skunk from his life. *Next time we meet there'll be no hesitation*, he thought. He raised a hand and pretended to shoot the guy, muttering, 'Bang, bang, you're dead, scumbag!'

'What's that you said?'

'Just thinking aloud is all, Marshal,' he replied. 'I was hoping to leave here today.'

'Don't matter none,' shrugged Jukes, offering him a cigar. 'There are enough charges listed on the indictment to see this skunk hang three times over.' He then handed over a credit note to secure the $500 reward from the bank without a qualm. 'Don't you go spending it all at once.' A half-smile accompanied the light-hearted comment. 'Except in the Saguero saloon over yonder. I'm a part-owner.'

'That's good advice, Marshal,' Crado chuckled, then punched the air as he left the jail. 'I aim to do just that.'

Affecting a well-earned swagger, he crossed the street to celebrate his good fortune.

He had now become a fully-fledged bounty hunter. The marshal's badge together with the accreditation certificate signed by Jack Banner would be retained, though, only to be used if and when the need arose.

Three down, one to go. The capture of Purvis would complete Crado's task of retribution. Only then could he resume his pursuit of that dream so abruptly cut short in the Brazos Valley. Following a couple of drinks and a well-earned meal in the Saguero, the man-hunter rode out of Williamsburg. His direction was towards the setting sun.

Weeks turned into months as he tracked the elusive neck-stretching critter. First through the Mogollon uplands of New Mexico, then into Arizona and across the bleak expanse of the Natanes Plateau. His destination was ever westward.

Each time he learned of the skunk's last known whereabouts, there was another robbery, another killing added to the latest dodger. Yet every time he figured to be closing the net, the varmint disappeared.

Crado was secretly pleased that Purvis was still a fugitive. Two grand had grown to three, which was a mighty tempting pot. All the same, it was a frustrating period, and he harboured no doubts that others of his ilk would be equally keen to secure the expanding reward.

4

Beaten to the Punch

Now, some five years later and still no closer to catching up with his quarry, Crado Bluestone was standing outside the Cactus Wren in Black Mesa.

Barely a thought had been given to the capture of his quarry for some considerable time. The guy appeared to have disappeared into thin air, but Crado was pretty sure the skunk had not been brought in. News of that sort would have surely filtered down the grapevine.

And then, out of the blue, the skunk's ugly mush had once again swum into view. It had happened periodically for no accountable reason. Perhaps it was due to his habit of checking on saddles. He stuffed the odious picture to the back of his mind, for now there was another fish waiting to be hauled in.

The bounty hunter's ice blue gaze dropped to the poster clutched in his hand. His brow furrowed in thought.

'Now where are you hiding out, *hombre?*' he muttered to himself, brushing back a stray lock of sandy hair.

'Buy me a drink, fella, and I could be the one to enlighten you.' Dulcet feline tones jerked Crado from his reverie. He turned to face the speaker.

Clad in a fancy dress that revealed more than it concealed stood a much more appealing picture in red and black. An elegant coiffure of auburn tresses decorated with a white bow was most assuredly not for regular daytime wear. The lady in question appeared to read his thoughts.

'I'm just about to perform on stage inside,' she said, guiding the newcomer through the batwing doors. 'Stick around after the show and you could learn something.' She left him with a sly wink that hinted at more than just information should he play his cards right.

Crado tipped his hat and wandered over to the bar. He ordered a beer and enquired as to the identity of the singer who was now stepping up on to the stage at the rear of the saloon to thunderous applause.

'Her name is Mirabelle Leguarde,' the barman declared with a proud flourish. 'The boss brought her in all the way from Flagstaff. She's only been here a week and has already doubled our takings.'

'She didn't sound French to me when we met outside,' replied the cynical drinker.

'Who cares where she's from?' The dreamy-eyed barkeep shrugged. 'Great singers are hard to come by. Especially in a berg like Black Mesa.' The mellifluous cadence drifting across the smoke-filled room had every eye glued to the stage. 'You gotta admit it, mister. This gal is one of the best.' Crado settled down with the rest of the mesmerized throng to enjoy the show.

The barman was right. Mirabelle Leguarde was one fine warbler.

Having finished her set to enthusiastic cries for more, the singer assured her audience that she would be back later with more of the latest tunes. Acknowledging the accolades bestowed on her as she passed through the crowds of drinking men, Mirabelle deftly fended off pawing hands. She was an expert at deflecting lecherous proposals without causing offence.

Like the others in the room, Crado was dazzled by the lady's magnetic aura. Reaching his side she called across to the bartender.

'I'll have my usual, Charlie. Put it on this gentleman's tab.' Lowered eyelids and a pouting smile challenged Crado to object. He nodded across. 'And I'll have another beer.'

The two exchanged knowing looks as the drinks were poured. Nothing more was said until both their hands were occupied. Crado raised his glass.

'To a brilliant performance Miss . . . erm . . . Leguarde?'

The implied insinuation brought a cheeky grin to the girl's painted features.

'It's my stage name. Elsie Perkins from Butte, Montana doesn't quite have the same ring, don't you think?' She held his gaze defiantly. 'Mister . . . ?'

'The name's Crado,' he replied. 'And a smart cookie like you has probably worked out by now that I am by profession what they call a bounty hunter. So perhaps you could explain what you know about the whereabouts of this dude.' He tapped the face on the poster. Mirabelle snorted.

'An ugly brute but one with a silky tongue. A devious scumbag as well.' One of Crado's eyebrows lifted, indicating his interest in her continuing. 'The rat made me think he was a top show-business impresario who had come down from Phoenix just to see

49

me. Promised me the world on a plate, he did. All for the measly sum of two hundred dollars to register my name with his agency.' She spat on the Wanted dodger. 'And, like a gullible fool, I fell for his slick patter hook, line and sinker.'

'Much as I sympathize with your predicament, honey,' interjected Crado, 'how does that help me catch up with him?'

'Once the money had been handed over, we celebrated with a few drinks up in my room. More than a few, in fact.'

Crado's arched regard hinted that he was well aware of what she was implying.

The singer's reaction was a stiff rebuttal of the unspoken accusation as she hurried on.

'Hold up there, mister!' She sniffed, tossing her head back. 'What sort of a girl do you think I am?'

Instantly repentant, the guy quickly raised a hand in apology. He had no wish to antagonize this dame before she had spilled the beans. Mirabelle graciously condescended to accept the olive branch.

'Sure, he tried his hand,' she continued. 'But I made it crystal-clear this was purely a business association and nothing more. It was the chance to improve my career, so I was gentle as a lamb with the put-down. But the drink had loosened his tongue enough to let me know where he was headed when he left here.'

'And what made you figure that he was a charlatan and not the real thing?' asked the puzzled bounty hunter.

The girl slung back the rest of her fancy cocktail and ordered another before replying. Crado voiced no objection.

'Next day Judge Benedict pinned up that Wanted dodger. When I saw it, the likeness was uncanny.' Once again she peered down at the face of El Vengador. 'Those shifty eyes, the slack mouth and the Mexican accent. They all should have rung alarm bells. But he was well-dressed and knew how to deliver a line. A born confidence trickster. I blame myself entirely.'

'So how about sharing this vital piece of information?' Crado quietly suggested. 'I've bought the drink, two in fact. Now it's your turn.'

'I said that I *might* divulge what I know.' She paused purposefully to consider what to reveal, if anything. 'Seems to me that a share of that reward will go a long way to loosening my tongue. After all, I am two hundred bucks down on account of that slimeball. So what do you say? Do we have a deal?' Mirabelle stuck out a hand to seal the agreement.

Crado was momentarily taken aback by the girl's sudden change of tactics. This needed thinking on.

'And what would you consider a fair share, Miss Leguarde?' He deliberately laid stress on the girl's stage name.

'I was figuring half would be a good offer.'

Crado's mouth crinkled in dissent. 'No way, lady. I'm doing all the dangerous work to catch this desperado. If'n you'd read the whole dodger properly you'd see that he's a thief and killer as well as a fraudster. A real mean dude. I'll give you three hundred. That's an extra hundred on top of your original loss. A good profit for doing nothing.'

Now it was Mirabelle's turn to look aggrieved. Frowns and grimaces marred her beguiling allure. 'Buy me another of these fine cocktails and I'll think about it.'

Crado sighed. This gal was a tough cookie as well the most alluring female he had ever laid eyes on. A taut silence followed as the girl slowly sipped her drink.

'So what's it to be, lady,' grunted the impatient man-hunter.

'Without my piece of vital information, you'll be scrabbling around in the dark looking for this skunk. Could take you weeks or longer.' She looked long and hard into Crado's incredibly magnetic blue eyes. For a moment she was tempted to accept his offer. Then the moment passed. 'Half it is, or no deal.'

'You strike a hard bargain, Miss Leguarde.' The reply was laced with a blend of irritation and admiration. 'OK, it's a deal.' They shook on the agreement.

'That's a sound decision, Crado. And maybe, when you bring the toerag in there'll be a bonus you weren't expecting.' The charismatic flutter of long eyelashes brought a flush to the bounty hunter's cheeks. 'Always assuming you keep your part of the agreement.' Her eyebrows lifted playfully. But she didn't wait for a reaction. 'See you later, big boy. Sorry to leave so soon, but I still have to earn my living.'

'So which direction is this greaser headed?' Crado asked, grasping her arm as she made to leave.

'Oh yes, I almost forgot. Silly me.' She giggled at her deliberate oversight.

'He's headed for Tucson. Ask Charlie about the best route to take.'

She tossed down the rest of the cocktail, then sashayed over to the stage, much to the obvious delight of the crowd.

Crado listened to the first song before leaving. He knew that whatever happened in the next few days, he would be back to visit the Cactus Wren, and Miss Leguarde in particular. Once outside, his whole attention reverted to the business of catching up with the colourful personage known as *El Vengador*.

A brief conflab with Charlie the bartender had elicited a vital piece of information regarding a short cut to Tucson. It began a mile south of Black Mesa. Turn off the main trail at Needle Bluff. Traversing the Mescal badlands by way of Tortilla Pass, a lone rider could chop three days off the regular stagecoach journey. But he would need to be well provisioned. It was a much rougher trail, dry as a temperance hall, and once used by the Apache before they moved north into the White Mountains.

Crado was assuming that the wanted outlaw was unaware of the short cut. Nor was he likely to be in much of hurry so would have taken the regular trail anyway. After packing extra water bottles he called in at the livery stable on the edge of town to feed and water his horse before setting out on the hazardous journey.

He experienced no difficulty in picking up the thin trail that started behind the spindly upthrust of Needle Bluff. Charlie had been right. It certainly was a rough trail. Thankfully no stray Indians were to be spotted.

On the afternoon of the second day out he was brought to a sudden halt by the crackle of gunfire. It was coming from the far side of a line of splintered rocks. Tethering his horse, Crado drew his pistol and hustled up to the crest.

Gingerly he peered down on to the scene of what looked like a one-sided gunfight. Three men had cornered a third up against a vertical cliff face. The lone adversary had to be *El Vengador*, and he was trapped with no way out. His horse had drifted away and was idly munching on a clump of bunch grass. Not only that, his rifle was still in the saddle boot. A single handgun was no match for three rifles.

It was only a matter of time before they picked him off. The Wanted dodger was of the *Dead-or-Alive* sort. Crado immediately recognized one of the assailants as a rival in the bounty-hunting profession. Like Crado, Rowdy Slag Bassett usually worked alone. He must have signed up a pair of helpers to ensure success. Bassett was known for bringing his marks in strung over a saddle. That appeared to be his objective on this occasion as well.

Crado's brow furrowed in annoyance. Being beaten to the punch did not sit well on his broad shoulders. He needed to even the score. That meant removing the opposition. Much as he preferred offering his adversaries the chance to surrender, this occasion did not merit such a magnanimous gesture.

Quickly he slid back down to secure his own long rifle. His preference was for the Remington rolling block with an extended barrel for long-range shooting. Although a single-shot weapon, he regarded it as being superior to the carbines these guys were toting. Winchester repeaters could snap off more shots, but they lacked range, an essential trait in the current circumstances. Also, they easily broke when roughly handled.

Credo took up his position behind a rock overlooking the gunmen. He slid a round into the breech and took careful aim, waiting until one of the bushwhackers raised his head. The booming roar echoed across the rocky desert. It was a perfect shot. The guy threw up his arms and slumped over with a .45 calibre slug in his head.

Shocked at this sudden twist of fortune, Rowdy Slag and his buddy ducked down. Another shot from the Remington sent a hat spinning skywards. But the telltale puff of smoke had revealed Crado's position. His two opponents began peppering the ridge, but their bullets fell short.

'You'll need to do a sight better than that,' Crado hooted, deliberately taunting the other bounty killer. A bout of acerbic laughter was greeted by more impotent shots. 'This is how it should be done,' he snapped. A single blast took the second man in the chest when he tried shifting position. 'Now it's down to you and me, Rowdy.'

'Who in tarnation are you, mister?' enquired a thoroughly rattled Slag Bassett.

'The name is Crado Bluestone. Maybe you've heard of me.'

Silence followed as Bassett absorbed the disclosure. He certainly did know the infamous man hunter, but by reputation only. Although they had never met, Crado's name was legendary among those who made their living on the fringes of the law.

'We can work this out, Bluestone,' said Bassett. 'This guy is worth a cool thousand. How about us sharing it out, fifty-fifty? That's fair, ain't it?'

'Too late, Rowdy,' came back the breezy response. 'I already made plans with another party. And it don't include you.' A raucous guffaw struck fear into Bassett's heart. 'Guess it's show time. You ready to meet your Maker?'

Another bullet zipped past Bassett's ear. Remaining in his present position was not an option. There was no chance of sneaking up on the other jasper without exposing himself: there was only one course of action left open. He took it. Head down, he backed off to where the three horses were tethered.

Rowdy Slag might have been a cocky braggart full of hot air when holding a full house, but he was no fool. He knew when to fold his hand. Better to run and stay healthy than play against a loaded deck, especially when Crado

Bluestone was holding all the best cards.

Crado let him go. He was a ruthless man hunter, but no backshooter. A couple more bullets singeing the villain's hair speeded him on his way. Satisfied that no further interference was likely from that quarter, Crado turned his attention to the trapped greaser.

5

Monstrous Capture

The wanted felon was not about to surrender easily. He had heard the exchanges of gunfire and knew that danger still lurked in the rocks. Although one threat had been eradicated, another still remained. He buzzed a couple of slugs up towards the ridge.

'Nobody is going to take *El Vengador* alive,' he called out. 'I can wait you out, *hombre*. The dark of night will soon be upon us. Then it will be you who should be afraid. One against one are odds that I like.' A mirthless cackle bounced off the cliff face behind where the The Avenger was hidden.

It was true. Crado had no wish to be trading lead with this slippery jasper after sundown when his current advantage would be effectively neutralized.

Now was the time to change tactics, and he knew just how to flush that smug good-for-nothing waster out of his cover.

This area of Arizona was well known for a particular creature that no man wanted to encounter close up. There were likely to be plenty around here, skulking in the rocks. They tended to hide in dark hollows during the hot hours of daylight.

Such were the sinister gila monsters. Pink and black, these horny lizards had acquired a mythical status among the local Apache tribes, who claimed that their breath could kill. Certainly the creature's deadly bite was no figment of the imagination. Its venom was just as lethal as that of the ubiquitous rattle-snake.

South of the border in Old Mexico, the natives had likewise invested the gila's cousin, the beaded lizard, with similar legendary abilities. The trapped Mexican bandit would doubtless be well-acquainted with these fables. Crado meant to take full advantage of that primal fear.

As the fierce heat had died away, now was the time that gilas ought to be appearing. Unlike the rattler, they were not normally rapacious towards humans. So Crado knew that if he kept still and quiet he should have no trouble capturing one by the tail.

He emptied the sack containing his spare duds and settled down to await developments. Ten minutes later a scrabbling close by drew his attention to a fully grown specimen as it emerged from its lair. The key was to avoid those deadly jaws. Once they snapped shut, nothing would prise them apart. Extreme care was consequently required in effecting the capture. He soon had the ungainly creature safely stashed away inside the sack. It thrashed around inside for a bit before settling down.

Now all he had to do was move around to the top of the cliff behind his quarry. Ten minutes later Crado peered over the rim of the mesa. From this position all he could see was the guy's boot sticking out from behind a boulder. It was enough. Gingerly manoeuvring the sack into position, he shook the contents out. The writhing creature tumbled down, landing next to the exposed leg.

A cry of terror tore the silence apart as the Mexican became aware of the imminent danger close by. He immediately tried to scramble out of the reach of those lethal, vicelike jaws. Maddened by its recent incarceration, the reptile lunged at the nearest movement. Its prey was lucky to escape that initial attack. When threatened, the gila monster will vigorously defend itself, as this one did now.

El Vengador's natural impulse was to escape, but. luck and the devil were not on his side. He hurled himself from the confined space behind the rocks and out into the open, but that was just where Crado wanted him. Once the reptile had lost sight of its prey it scuttled away. The panting survivor now realized that another danger loomed, equally threatening. A bullet dug into the ground beside his feet.

'Stay right where you are, *muchacho*!' came the blunt order from the cliff face behind. 'Shuck your gunbelt and remove them boots. You ain't going no place until I'm good and ready.'

The outlaw hesitated.

'You hear me, greaser?' Another slug clipped the Mexican's boot heel, urging him to comply. Keeping a gimlet eye on the helpless felon, Crado made his way down to ground level.

'It seems that El Vengador is very popular today,' the bandit declared with a somewhat nonchalant acceptance of his predicament. Then he saw the dodger that his captor was studying. 'Hey, gringo, let me see that.' He held out a hand. A grimace meant to signify approval twisted the stubble-coated face.

'Is good likeness, don't you think,' he bragged, twirling the droopy moustache that graced his upper lip like a fat hairy worm. 'A handsome fellow, am I not?'

Crado scoffed. 'I was figuring the same thing . . . the likeness, I mean. Although from where I'm standing you look more like an unmade bed. A rumpled, untidy mess in dire need of an overhaul.' He lit a cigar and deliberately puffed a couple of perfect smoke rings at the sorry specimen. 'This should help dull the odious reek from that grubby poncho. How any gal could cotton to you is a mystery.'

El Vengador huffed and snorted indignantly. 'How you say such a thing? It is a foul insult to my *machismo*. I have *señoritas* by the score falling at my feet. And my war bag contains a full set of fancy duds.'

'With an ugly mush like that they must need spectacles, or are well beyond the marriage stakes.' Crado chuckled at his own witty repartee. Then his face clouded over. 'Anyway, far as I'm concerned your value is far more important to me than your looks.

A thousand bucks will go a long way to refreshing my bank balance.'

'What was that I heard you tell Rowdy Slag about another party involved?' The prisoner's face displayed his puzzlement.

'A certain lady back in Black Mesa was less than happy when you tricked her with that fake promise of fame and fortune. I made her one I intend to keep.' His fixed stare indicated that he meant business. 'And that was to bring you in and share the reward with her.'

'Aaaaaah, *si*!' the Mexican drawled nodding. 'The *exquisita* Mirabelle Leguarde. Now there is one *bella señorita*.'

'I ain't got no argument with you there, *amigo*.' Crado's eyes misted over at the thought of his next remark. 'And that bonus she hinted at sure sounds inviting.'

The Mexican grunted. 'And all El Vengador gets in return is a date with the hangman. Not a very good exchange, *hombre*.'

Crado shrugged. 'That's the way the

cookie crumbles, as they say. If'n the boot was on the other foot, I'm sure you would do the same. Tricking her with your silky chat was a bad move. A very bad move. Guess you ain't never heard the saying about the fury of a woman scorned.'

A sly twist to the Mexican's slash of a mouth hinted that there could be another solution to his dilemma.

'You gotten something to say?' asked Crado, keeping the brigand closely covered with his revolver.

'There is perhaps another way for us to settle this little problem, as *buenos amigos*.'

Crado's lazy peepers lifted, indicating that the guy should continue. 'In your case, buddy, I wouldn't have said it was a minor issue.'

The Mexican hawked out a manic guffaw. 'You are one cool dude, gringo. But if you listen carefully to my proposition, we can both enjoy much *felicidad*.'

Crado eyed him askance. 'I'm happy

enough already. Five hundred bucks coming my way when I've handed you over says so.'

The Mexican shrugged off this witty rejoinder and launched into his proposal.

'I am in possession of valuable knowledge that can lead us both to a fortune in hidden money.' He paused to study the other man's reaction. Crado's gaze remained even, devoid of expression. The bandit was not deterred.

'And El Vengador is prepared to share it with you. Much better than a measly half-share of my reward. So what you say? No woman is worth turning down such an offer.'

Crado posed his own question instead. 'I hope you're not expecting me to help you steal this fabled treasure trove. My job is to hunt down bad guys like you and deliver them to the authorities. According to my information, you need to seriously consider the wicked profession you have chosen.' Realizing what he had said, Crado burst out laughing.

'What is so funny, gringo?' Irritation traced a path across the Mexican's leathery features.

'My mistake, buddy.' The man-hunter couldn't resist deriding his puzzled prisoner. 'The choice has already been made for you, hasn't it?'

'There is no danger involved, I assure you.' Desperation to avoid a certain necktie party urged the Mexican to insist his proposal was genuine. 'This money is buried in a secret place that only I know. There is enough stashed away to enable both of us to enjoy a good time for years to come.'

The wanted man looked at his captor, sure that such an offer would not be refused. He was assuming that the bounty hunter, like many of his ilk, measured his rules of procedure solely in monetary terms. Often that might well have been the case, but sadly for the bandit, on this occasion it was an erroneous assumption. In any case, Crado didn't believe a word of the greaser's claim, seeing it as just a last-ditch attempt to secure his freedom.

The poker-faced bounty hunter sat still, his gun arm rigid as a branding-iron. When at last he spoke, it was in plain, blunt terms.

'You underestimate me, pal. Mirabelle would be worth turning you in even without a reward. Now, on your face so's I can fasten you up good and tight,' he rasped. 'We'll stay here the night, and set out at first light . . . ' he paused for effect, 'back to Black Mesa and the hangman's reach.'

The irate Mexican bandit realized that his sure-fire gambit for freedom had alighted upon deaf ears. He rained down vitriolic curses upon his captor, until Crado was forced to gag him.

★   ★   ★

A couple of days later they arrived back in Black Mesa where Crado delivered the wanted outlaw to Judge Benedict.

The legal eagle was taken aback by the arrival of this unexpected guest.

'I thought he'd be well across the border by now. How did you catch up with him so quick?'

'Fortunately for me the guy found himself delayed on the trail.'

He ignored the judge's raised eyebrows that sought a more detailed explanation. Any further disclosure was best left unspoken while two other jiggers this close to the town were having their bones picked clean by scavengers. Instead he asked the question uppermost in his mind.

'When's the hanging likely to take place?'

'Tomorrow morning after I've conducted the trial in the Cactus Wren,' Benedict replied. 'Will you be there?'

Black Mesa justice was swift and certain. In the circumstances the verdict would be a foregone conclusion.

Crado remained silent. His extended hand waited to receive the reward money. Benedict willingly obliged. The recipient made a special point of counting every last dollar in front of the portly official.

'It's all there,' huffed the pompous toad. 'Don't you trust me?'

The waspish question was met with an equally forthright response.

'What do you think, Judge?' Crado laid an emphasis on the title that was intended to indicate his scornful view of the lawman. 'I've been tricked too often by *honest* lawmen in the past.' He continued silently shuffling the wad of greenbacks. 'But I'm pleased to inform you that you, sir, are in the clear.' The venomous grimace that followed this declaration sent a shiver down the judge's spine. 'So I'll bid you good day.'

After pocketing the reward he headed across the street for the share-out.

His arrival had been timed to perfection. Mirabelle Leguarde was just finishing her spot on stage. After acknowledging the spirited applause, she noticed the bounty hunter standing in the doorway. A fleeting smile accompanied her delicately inclined gesture for the newcomer to follow her upstairs.

Once they were inside her room, she fell into his arms. No preamble, no preliminary small talk. The promised bonus was available with no provisos attached. Although taken by surprise at the girl's now brazen manner, Crado allowed himself to be swept along by the torrent of mingled lust and gratitude. He was not to be disappointed.

Nor was the donor. Both parties relished to the full all that could be drawn from the intimate coupling. The age-old ritual was practised in all its sensual glory.

When they both finally surfaced, gasping for breath, Crado needed a smoke to calm his jangled nerves.

'I ain't never earned a bonus like that before,' he eventually blurted out, accepting a glass of the champagne that had been cooling in an ice bucket.

'Plenty more where that came from if

you play your cards right,' the girl promised, snuggling up to this quietly handsome fireball. 'A girl has to settle down sometime. But only when the right man comes along who's willing to fill the void.' A forthright gaze from beneath the teasing arch of one eyebrow said more than any words could convey.

That boldly suggestive regard now placed Crado in a quandary. Never before had he met up with such a woman as Mirabelle Leguarde. Even in the darkened room, her beauty was evident. Much as he would have liked to accept the offer, there were too many other issues to be considered in his current situation.

Top of the list was his quest to hunt down Monk Purvis. There could be no hanging up his guns until that critter was dangling from a rope's end. Then there was the considered choice that Mirabelle had to make. Was she prepared to revert back to plain Elsie Perkins and live the mundane life of a housewife after all the adulation and excitement that her present occupation brought her?

They had only just met, were virtual strangers if truth be told. More water had to flow under the bridge before any decisions of such momentous proportions could be made. The bounty hunter's caution, the hesitation, was ill-concealed and noticeably apparent to the singer.

'Guess you aren't as eager as I figured,' she sighed, clearly vexed by the man's now cool attitude. The rejection of her transparent proposal was not what she had expected or wanted.

'When a gal lays her feelings on the line like I've just done, it comes as a deeply wounding humiliation when the guy she throws her cap at turns his back on her,' she wailed.

'It's not like that,' Crado hurried to reassure this beautiful woman. 'I'm flattered beyond words, believe me. And I'd love to accept . . . ' He turned away, trying to find some explanation that would mollify her.

'So what's the giant-sized *but* you're gonna drop in my lap?'

'To begin with, we barely know each other. We're strangers who have been thrown together by circumstance. Not a great way to start a life of domestic bliss.' He then handed over the girl's share of the reward. 'Blood money was how we first met up. It's the way I earn a living. Just as singing is your business. We need time to find out if it will work, see if'n we're well-matched. There'll likely have to be compromises.'

Mirabelle nodded. She clutched his hand.

'You're right,' she said. 'Guess I was carried away by the moment.'

'And there is something else.'

She threw him a poignant look of concern. He turned up the oil lamp on the bedside table, then his fingers traced along the purple ridged disfigurement.

The girl sucked in a sharp intake of breath. Shock was written across her distressed countenance.

'Who did that?' she gasped out.

Not having seen the awful scarring during their previous night's bedchamber activities, she found the sight all the more shocking. Other things had been occupying both mind and body in the darkened room. Yet even to the most naive intelligence, it was clear that the mutilation was the result of a hangman's rope.

'What sort of monster could leave a man with such a cross to bear?'

'One by the name of Monk Purvis,' he snarled out in a rancid growl. 'So you see. Before I could even consider settling down, I have to find the rat. It's him or me, no half-measures. Sooner or later I'll run him down. But when that will be is in the lap of the gods.' He shrugged, got to his feet and quickly dressed.

'Do you have to go right away?' she implored him. 'I still have another week here before heading for my next engagement in Globe.'

Crado shook his head. 'Best I go now. No tearful goodbyes. The longer I stay the harder it will be to break away. You do understand, don't you?'

She gave a gulp, a half-smile tinged with sadness and a brief nod of accord as he moved over to the door.

'But make no mistake,' he added, turning back to look at her, 'when my job is done I'll come searching for you. All I can hope is that you ain't gotten tired of waiting and been swept away by some more deserving jasper. There again, you might decide that it was a rash proposal after all. Once a bounty hunter, always . . . '

He left the clear message unfinished. Could a man of his calling ever truly find peace? Only time would tell. Then he was gone. Mirabelle threw herself back onto the bed and cried until no more tears would flow.

6

Change of Plan

The next morning witnessed a particularly good turn out to enjoy the proceedings in the Cactus Wren. This was the first occasion that Black Mesa had hosted the trial of an outlaw matching El Vengador's notoriety. The main body of the room was full. Only the central area was left clear. There a chair was placed on which the wobegone outlaw was seated. Two hefty guards were posted on either side.

On the stage were seated the so-called jury with an empty chair draped in red velvet in the centre. This was clearly for Judge Benedict, when he deigned to make an entrance. The saloon owner welcomed the occasion. It was definitely good for his prestige and standing in the community.

The muted conversation was suddenly curtailed when an official voice announced the start of the proceedings.

'All stand for the trial of outlaw and killer, El Vengador. Judge Roy Benedict presiding.'

There followed a shuffling of chairs, then the whole room fell silent. One of the guards dragged the laggard prisoner upright.

Affecting his most dignified guise, the man in charge entered the room and strode purposefully across to his throne. He paused to survey the solemn gathering. He gave a loftily imperious twitch, meant to signify to all and sundry exactly who was calling the shots here. When he finally sat, everyone else followed suit.

Crado had slid in through the front door just before the judge's arrival. He parked himself at the back, behind the wheel of fortune.

Evidence related to the killing of the mine-owner's son was presented by the man himself. Chess Thurwell gave an impassioned dialogue about the loss of his only kin.

On various occasions during the questioning, the judge had to call for order. 'This court will be cleared if you jaspers don't control yourselves.'

The vigilance committee of tough miners sitting on either side of the judge left the gathering in no doubt who was in charge here. Muttering and grumbling like a bunch of chastened school kids, the crowd quickly simmered down.

Thurwell's submission was supported by the one guard who had survived the attack. Angry glares swung towards the prisoner. Gasps of anguish followed when he described how he had fought off the brigand after the accused had killed his comrade, the mine-owner's son. But luckily the gold shipment had been saved. This last declaration received a round of cheering which Judge Benedict magnanimously permitted. After some moments an arrogant lift of his hand curtailed the outburst and brought instant silence.

'Has the accused anything to say in his defence?' the judge asked, peering down his beaky snout at the miserable felon.

Once again El Vengador was dragged to his feet. Then the outlaw assumed an ugly, almost intimidating posture, silencing the gabble in the courtroom. All at once he looked a different man, taller, more self-assured. As he assumed his most disdainful mien his black-hearted gaze panned the room.

'This is not a trial,' he snarled out. '*Es un farsante de aupa, una burla!*'

The judge turned to the foreman of the jury. 'What did he say?'

The man looked uncomfortable, embarrassed. He swallowed then stammered out a muttered translation.

'H-he s-said . . . 'It is just a big sham, a mockery!'' Then he sat down quickly trying to hide behind his fellow jurors.

'What?' The haughty adjudicator's face turned purple as if he was about to have a convulsion. 'How dare anyone claim this is anything but a properly convened court. We may not as yet have territorial backing, but I am the law here and what I say goes.' Benedict did not appear to realize that he was in essence concurring with the prisoner's own indictment.

One of the guards picked up on the judge's fury and cuffed the prisoner around the head. El Vengador fell back into his seat.

No further witnesses were called. So that was it. The trial was over.

'The jury will now convene to decide on its verdict,' the judge announced, having regained his composure. 'And we know what that will be, eh?' He smirked.

Only six good men and true had been deemed necessary. They grouped themselves in a circle to discuss the evidence. Five minutes passed before the judge enquired in a loud stentorian voice, 'Has the jury reached a verdict yet?'

'We have, your honour,' declared the foreman.

'And what is your verdict?'

Abner Winkleman stood up. This was the store clerk's one moment of fame in his mundane life and he intended milking it to the limit. All eyes were fixed on him. Only the prisoner's were lowered. He knew exactly what the verdict would be. Time stood still in the Cactus Wren. Only when Judge Benedict snorted out a rebuke did the preening foreman declare, 'Guilty, your honour.'

A universal exhaling of breath from the tense mass of humanity seemed to disturb the pall of cigar smoke hanging in the air.

'Prisoner will stand,' the judge rapped out. 'You, El Vengador, have been found guilty of murder and other crimes by a jury of your peers. You will be taken forthwith outside, there to be hanged by the neck until you are dead. And may the Good Lord have mercy on your worthless soul.' He spat on the straw-covered floor. 'Take the bastard out and string him up.'

86

The trial had lasted no more than an hour. As expected, the outcome was a foregone conclusion, but even Crado was caught unawares by the speed with which the sentence was to be carried out. He had figured at least another day in the hoosegow before the grim deed took place.

Sleep the previous night had eluded him. Leaving Mirabelle in such a pitiful manner had forced him to question his motives. Was he doing the right thing? Should he go back and beg her forgiveness? It was a situation still unresolved when the shock announcement came.

Another idea was also vying for dominance in Crado's disjointed thinking. One that demanded an immediate resolution. The prisoner was being hustled outside to meet his finale, followed by the excited crowd of spectators.

Keeping a low profile, the bounty hunter headed for the stairs. A quick glance round reassured him that all eyes were elsewhere. He bypassed Mirabelle's room and headed for the open veranda on the second floor, overlooking the place of execution. The hanging tree stood in the middle of the plaza. The noose had already been put in place in expectation of the *right* verdict.

Crado gave thanks that he had tethered his own horse on the hitching rail immediately below where he now crouched.

Unfortunately, his rifle was still in its saddle boot. He would have to place his trust in the Colt Frontier. That entailed moving along to the end of the veranda to get within the gun's effective range. There he waited while the guest of honour at the necktie party was mounted on his horse and led across to meet his doom. There was no struggling on his part, no final pleas for mercy.

Crado could only give credit where it was due, respecting the guy's courage. Few others would have been so accepting of their fate.

As the noose was slung around the

condemned man's neck, awful flashes of recall fizzed through Crado's brain. He pushed them away, concentrating his entire being on what had to be done. He rested the barrel of the revolver on the wooden safety rail. Images of Jack Banner being in a similar situation now shouldered their way forward. The same dead, hopeless look on the victim's face was doubtless what the Texas Ranger perceived before he pulled the trigger.

The only difference here was that Crado was not going to wait until The Avenger had almost choked his life away.

No pity or generous regard for the Mexican's well-being entered into the decision. It was a pragmatic view that the crowd might decide to hasten the proceedings. Chess Thurwell, the mine owner, was generously paying for a free bar once the hanging was completed. Free booze was apt to make the regular patrons impatient for a rapid send-off.

The judge's arm was once again

grabbing at the clouds, ready to give the order. Crado timed his shot to perfection, confident of his aim even with a handgun. The loud blast echoed around the plaza as the rope was shredded. Panic gripped the spectators, who ran for cover. A follow-up shot lifted Judge Benedict's stovepipe from his head. Uproar and mayhem ensured that the rescue was accomplished without hindrance.

Crado leapt over the balustrade and landed in his saddle.

'Shift your ass, Vengador!' he shouted, vigorously urging the stunned victim, still aboard his own horse, to dig his heels in. 'I'll cover you.' Another fusillade of shots kept heads firmly out of sight until the two fugitives were galloping hell for leather down the main street.

Only then did some of the more enterprising individuals try to stop them. Perhaps it was the nonappearance of free beer that stimulated their actions rather than civic loyalty.

Slugs buzzed around the heads of the fleeing fugitives like angry hornets. Luckily none found its mark. Within seconds, the two men had rounded a bend at the far end of Black Mesa and disappeared from view.

But the danger was nowhere near past yet. Flight to safety was essential. Crado cut the bonds securing the rescued man's wrists.

'You any notion of a good place to hide in these parts, *amigo?*' he asked, keeping his head down. 'I'm a stranger round here.'

Totally reanimated following his shock deliverance, the desperado replied, 'Head straight out into the desert and keep going. They'll follow for a spell, then give up. Most folks reckon it's a death warrant to cross the Sonora.' He chuckled heartily. The unleashing of tension in him was palpable. 'But I know different.'

The reason for Crado's change of heart had not as yet become a burning issue. At that moment, freedom and escape from retribution were a priority. They galloped on. Frequent looks along their back trail showed a plume of dust. The chase was on. But did the Mexican have it right? Only time would tell.

'Best we slow up to conserve the nags,' Crado advised, reining down to a steady canter. The outlaw followed suit. 'How far is this secret hideaway? It looks like nothing but blistering sand and sagebrush far as the eye can see.'

'It is all an illusion.' El Vengador tapped his head. A meaningful smirk hinted that he had mysterious distractions in mind for their pursuers. 'On far side of that ridge, we head due west. Then you see.'

Ten minutes later they crested the ridge from where a broad plateau of sandstone stretched away for upwards of a mile. A broken wall of rocks accompanied the right-hand edge of the flat tableland. The outlaw signalled a halt.

'This is where we play trick on those *bastardos*,' he growled. 'Come, follow me and prepare to be amazed.'

His manic laugh echoed across the bleak landscape. Then he led the way off the plateau. Behind the cluster of rocks the ground sloped down to where a series of interconnecting arroyos began.

'Flood waters running off the plateau have in past produced this maze of channels. With any luck, those *cretinos* will miss our turn-off on the plateau. With no tracks to follow, they will figure we have continued in a straight line to the far side.' The Mexican was now thoroughly enjoying himself. 'If by chance they do get lucky, it is *finito* for those who do not know way through. Many have tried and failed. Their bones now lie buried in the sand.'

'You sure have this all figured out, don't you?' Crado was genuinely impressed. It was going to make the plan he had formulated all the more credible.

'It is why I have escaped the long arm of American law for so long. Was bad luck running into Rowdy Slag Bassett. And then you came along, *amigo*. Was that good luck, or the devil's handshake?'

They rode on in silence for a while, the Mexican confidently leading the way. Very soon Crado was totally disoriented. Hard though he had tried to remember the various twists and turns, it proved an impossible task. Much to his discomfiture, he was now in the hands of this sly Mexican bandit. Once they were well into the labyrinth and relatively safe from pursuit, the Mexican fixed a sceptical eye upon his benefactor.

'So why you save my good self? You do not strike me as the charitable sort.'

'Let's find a spot to camp out for the night and maybe I'll tell you.' Crado was not saying anything more until he had worked out in his mind exactly how he wanted to play this situation. At the moment it was just an idea. A possibility of earning some easy money.

And El Vengador was the key to success.

After another half-hour the Mexican led them out of the arroyo in which they were travelling up on to the rim. There he signalled a halt.

'From here we can see if posse is on the ball, as you say.'

The site gave them an all-encompassing vista of the chaotic splay of water-eroded terrain. For ten minutes they waited, chewing on sticks of beef jerky, only spurring off when the outlaw was fully satisfied that his ruse had succeeded in their eluding their pursuers.

They reached the campsite an hour later in the heart of what had become known as Old Nick's Playground. It was actually a small abandoned miner's cabin beside a shallow creek. All the basic essentials were stored there.

The outlaw appeared to have been using it as a base of operations for some time. Not that he had made any significant profit from his nefarious ventures. A lone brigand is severely limited when it comes to the type of robberies he can successfully accomplish. His most recent foray proved the point.

That night after a frugal meal, he bemoaned his lack of success in his attempts to run a gang.

'Too many different characters, all wanting their say,' he grumbled. 'And too little reward after the share-out. The final straw came when one traitor decided to save his own skin and claim the reward by betraying the rest of us. That was end for me.'

'Were you caught?' Despite his disdain for the Mexican, Crado was intrigued.

'I only one to escape trap,' the outlaw hollered, banging his fist on the table. 'All rest were captured or killed.'

'What about the skunk that turned you in?'

A cold glint in the outlaw's narrowed gaze told Crado all he needed to know.

'Double-crossing rat!' he exclaimed.

'But I track him down, all the way back into Chihuahua. It took me a whole year.' Cackling like a demented scarecrow, he dramatically replayed the finale, mimicking a cut across the throat. 'Chico Alvarez is no longer with us. Since then I work alone. Less profitable but easier on nerves. *Bandidos Mejicanos* are ruthless and brave, but all want to be the boss.'

Sitting opposite each other in cane chairs, they each stared into the crackling logs of a fire burning in the stone hearth. The dancing flames were hypnotic. Smoke from their cigars diffused a certain ethereal quality into the atmosphere. Miles from the nearest piece of civilization, at that moment, Crado felt like he was living on another planet.

A silence had fallen upon the two men as each, unknown to the other, cast his thoughts back to similar situations. In Crado's case, however, the finale still eluded him. He added a snort of tequila to his coffee and puffed on the fine Havana cigar before voicing another query that had sprung to mind.

'So what about that elusive cache of dough you were trying to buy me off with? Is that just a dream you invented to avoid a neck-stretching?'

The outlaw sighed. 'No invention I can assure you. But a long story, and one that will only be revealed when I know that I can really trust you. It is how I became the notorious *bandido* known as El Vengador. Perhaps if we are to become partners you should call me by real name, which is Juan Batista.'

The bounty hunter nodded. 'Pleasure to meet you, Juan. Crado Bluestone at your service. At least . . . I hope our association is going to be profitable, if not exactly a pleasure.'

Batista studied his associate closely. A furtive leer spread across the stubbled acreage of his face.

'You are a strange *hombre*, Crado Bluestone. And that leads me to a puzzling concern that has been dancing round inside my head. Are you really *mi amigo?* Or just another cheating varmint like Alvarez?'

The look hardened. But it lacked menace as Crado had not as yet returned the guy's weaponry. Neither was he prepared to hand it back only to find it used against him.

'You're not the only one who needs convincing,' he drawled, taking another long draw on the cigar. 'Can I trust *you?*'

Batista stiffened in his chair. His hand gripped the table, his knuckles showing white. He looked ready to leap upon his confederate. Then just as quickly the ugly moment dissolved. A hearty bout of guffawing broke the tension.

'You are right. If we are to work well together, trust is important.'

Over the next few days the two unlikely partners settled into an accommodating relationship that wasn't exactly friendship, nor was it fractious, more a business arrangement. And that suited them both.

By the third day Crado was ready to reveal his plan. Sceptical and more than a little nervous at his part in the proceedings, Batista nonetheless agreed to go along with it.

7

Vanishing Act

One week later to the day, the two associates rode out of the hidden arroyo to begin their unique method of securing funds. Although an understanding had been reached during their stay in the cabin, real trust would take much longer to establish. But for Crado's plan to work, El Vengador was given no option but to place his life in the bounty hunter's capable hands.

Even after a week Batista was still not entirely convinced. Although it certainly appeared to be a good scheme, everything depended on the accuracy of Crado's shooting.

'Are you confident of being able to do the job every time?' Batista questioned for the umpteenth time. Even now, as they were riding away from the cabin, he was still chary regarding his partner's intentions. 'It's my life that will be hanging in balance.'

Crado couldn't resist a manic chortle at the unfortunate choice of words. Once again he gave the same reply. 'If'n I could do it with a pistol at twenty-five yards, I'm darned sure there'll be no problem with my Remington rolling block. And next time I'll be ready and in position. You worry too much.'

'Do I not have reason to fret? It is my neck on line, not yours.'

The Mexican's constant blathering was beginning to grate on Crado's nerves. He peered around. Perched on a flat rock just off to one side of the arroyo, a coyote was chewing on a dead gopher. He immediately dragged the rifle from its saddle boot and slammed the butt into his shoulder. Barely appearing to take aim he let fly. The animal stood no chance. It was knocked clear off its perch by the force of the shell.

'That answer your question, partner?'

he rasped, slotting a fresh round into the breech before returning the rifle to its housing. 'I'm the one who thought up this stunt. I want it to work just as much as you. And think of all that dough we're gonna make. On a regular basis, over and over again. No more worrying about getting your head shot off by stiff-necked shotgun guards. We can't lose. It's a sure-fire winner.'

The demonstration shut Batista's mouth. They rode on in silence.

The town selected for the initial foray was on the far side of the Pinaleno Mountains in the Gila Valley. Safford was a small berg similar in size to Black Mesa and known to have a town marshal with connections to the county seat at Globe. There was no telegraph service. Even better. Nobody would have yet learned about the outlaw's escape from justice. An ideal place to mount the initial trial of their macabre scam.

'I'll ride in first and look the place over, make sure there's a dodger with your name on it,' he said, giving the sleepy cluster the once-over. 'You stay here, and don't move. Have a smoke and keep calm. There's nothing to worry about.'

Crado left to enter the town from the blind side. Using the main trail could draw unwelcome attention. He wanted to remain invisible. Skirting a series of back lots and rundown shacks he approached the central plaza down a narrow alleyway. The square was characteristic of many towns in southern Arizona.

He dismounted and sidled out on to the main street. Nobody paid him any attention. Even a lone mutt chewing on a bone ignored him. The sign advertising the marshal's office could be seen two blocks west. With a steady gaze he panned the immediate vicinity. On the far side of the tree-girt plaza was a noticeboard advertising all manner of local activities soon to be taking place — horse-races, a barn dance, a sale of cut-price hay, homemade blueberry jam.

There, at the end, was that all-important dodger. Same picture but the price had indeed risen. Crado sucked in a lungful of air and rubbed his eyes to make sure he had not misread the new reward: two grand. He blew out a low whistle of approval.

That was all he needed to know. Peering round to make certain he was unobserved he tore the poster down, then quickly back-tracked. It had been a fleeting visit. In and out in the blink of an eye before disappearing like a wraith in the night.

When the infamous desperado was apprised of his new value, he cheered aloud.

'El Vengador must truly be feared in this part of the territory.'

Then, the grim reality of what he must do to earn his share struck home. It was a deeply unsettling prospect. To purposely allow himself to be set up for a hanging did not sit well. All of Crado's powers of persuasion were needed to bring him round. It took the better part of an hour until, finally, the outlaw was ready to play his role.

They headed down the hill, this time along the main trail. Crado tied his partner's hands and led the way, leading the other's horse.

'Remember to adopt a hangdog expression,' Crado threw back over his shoulder. 'This has to be convincing. Any suspicion by the tinstar and the curtain falls on a splendid opportunity to make some easy dough.'

'And my neck gets stretched,' burbled the outlaw morosely.

'That as well, I guess,' Crado graciously conceded. 'So it's up to you to make it look good. Be convincing. You sure had Mirabelle fooled. Make sure you have the same effect on these dudes.'

They drew rein outside the law office. The appearance of a man leading another tied to his saddle was an unusual sight in Safford. It attracted the attention of numerous passers-by. Keen to make a good impression, Crado dragged the dishevelled prisoner off his horse and snapped out:

'You've caused me a heap of trouble, El Vengador.' He shouted the words, making certain his accusation was audible and sounded suitably genuine. 'Two months I've been on your tail. Now you're gonna pay the price for all those robberies and killings.'

To lend substance to his wrath the bounty hunter cuffed the prisoner round the head. Batista fell to the ground, aiming a string of curses at his tormentor. His show of anger at the assault was exceptionally realistic. Perhaps because it was. He hadn't been expecting anything physical and it came as a shock.

'*Bastardo!*' he growled out. 'I get you for this one day.' He meant it. Crado's leery grin never faltered.

'Now shift your ass.' He manhandled the captive into the office, much to the surprise of Nate Sawyer.

'What's all this then?' he asked.

'Prisoner for you, Marshal, by the name of *El Vengador*.'

Sawyer's eyes lifted. 'Well, hush my boots!' he exclaimed. 'This guy's been on the wanted list for months. The authorities only put his price up last week.' He threw a somewhat chary look at the captor. 'You must be a bounty man, mister.'

'The name is Crado and I'm more than pleased to get this turkey off'n my hands.' He aimed a rancid snarl at his prisoner. 'Watch his every move, Marshal. That greaser's a real mean son of a bitch and slippery as a wet fish.'

The marshal pushed the outlaw into the cell block and locked him up.

'There is no jail in Arizona that can hold El Vengador,' the prisoner spat out. 'I am like ghost. Can walk through walls.' He chuckled maniacally, rattling the bars of his cage with a tin mug. 'Now how about some grub? That skunk of a bounty hunter only fed me scraps not fit for a dog.'

Nate Sawyer was chuckling himself

when he returned to the office.

'That critter sure hates you, Crado, and that's a durned fact. Can't say I blame him. The guy who brought him in ain't exactly gonna be his best buddy.'

'All that bothers me now, Marshal, is drawing my reward.' Crado fixed a self-assured peeper on to the young lawman. 'When do you expect that will be?'

'Too late in the day now,' the man replied. 'The bank closes at four o'clock. Get yourself a room at the hotel and I'll arrange it first thing in the morning.'

'And the trial, is that likely to be soon?' Crado tried not to appear over-interested. 'I just want to make sure this fella gets his just deserts is all.'

The marshal considered the question. 'I figure he'll have been tried, sentenced and hung by the weekend.'

'You seem mighty certain that he's guilty.'

'Ain't you?' Sawyer asked, rather

surprised that such an idea could be under consideration. 'Don't reckon you'd have tracked an innocent man for two months without being sure he'd done all the crimes listed on that dodger.'

'Guess your right there, Marshal.' Crado tipped his hat back. 'See you in the morning.' Then, in a voice loud enough for his confederate to hear, he asked, 'Can you recommend a good place to eat? I could sure murder a prime rib-eye steak with fried potatoes and green beans, all smothered with rich gravy. Some apple pie and fresh cream to follow would go down a treat. Makes me slaver just thinking on it.'

'You won't be disappointed with Betty Logan's Frontier Diner,' Sawyer replied without hesitation. 'It's a block east. Best hurry though. She soon gets filled up.'

'Much obliged, Marshal. I can hardly wait. You take good care of that critter in yonder cell block. Bread and water is good enough for him.' Crado could barely keep a straight face as he left the office — and he really was hungry. All they had eaten since leaving Old Nick's Playground was jerky washed down with tepid water.

Had the bounty man realized that Mexican humour did not equate to that of the American West, he would have held his tongue. *Machismo*, the glorification of masculinity, is a trait no Mexican worth his salt could allow to be dishonoured. Being made to look small, humiliated in the eyes of others, could not be allowed to go unchallenged. The outlaw had chosen well when adopting his pseudonym. A spark had been kindled that would smoulder and fester in his devious mind.

★   ★   ★

Time passed slowly for the prisoner over the next few days. But eventually the day of reckoning arrived.

As expected in these wild and remote

corners of the untamed western frontier, justice could be swift and brutal. Even where duly elected peace officers like Nate Sawyer were involved, the need for irrefutable proof of a man's culpability was often sidestepped. For due process to be followed it was often deemed sufficient if enough people assumed the accused prisoner was guilty as charged. With territorial judges in short supply and thinly spread throughout difficult terrain, judgment was often left in the hands of local officials.

Evidence in the form of a Wanted poster signed by the territorial governor was the seal of approval: irrefutable proof of guilt. It was, in effect, a death warrant for those deemed too much of a hazard to local affairs. In this regard the bounty hunter had become a mainstay, a principal bastion of effective law and order.

So, on the following Friday morning, the bandit known as El Vengador was led out of the jailhouse and over to a hastily built gallows. He was sweating, his breath emerging in nerve-shredded wheezes. The macho image so revered by his kind had disintegrated as the moment of truth approached. His panic-stricken gaze darted about, searching for his saviour.

But Crado was nowhere to be seen. During the intervening few days, he had carefully and covertly surveyed the town to find the ideal position from which to perform his magic trick. He had mulled over a list of important conditions needed to make his task simple yet effective.

So the morning of Friday found him lying prone behind the false front of a single-storey bootmaker's premises. His horse was saddled up and ready behind the store for a quick getaway.

Peering through a gap in the woodwork, he cranked up the Winchester rifle borrowed from his partner. On this occasion the single-shot Remington was unsuitable. A repeater was deemed necessary for what he had to do. He poked it carefully through the gap, lining the sight up on to the thick hank of rope swinging lazily in the light morning breeze.

All eyes were fixed upon the indication of the gruesome event about to be enacted below. Up on the rooftop, the gunman's only companions were a pair of curious quail.

'Come to enjoy the fun, guys?' he muttered under his breath before turning his attention back to the job in hand. He needed to get it just right.

A macabre hush had settled over the gathering of citizens in the centre of the plaza. The marshal placed the noose over the condemned man's head and pulled the knot tight.

Then he stepped back while the local preacher intoned a pious oration. As the Lord's representative on Earth he built up to a rousing climax in which the crowd joined with fervid enthusiasm. The final delivery was a sonorous invitation for Juan Batista, known as El Vengador, to make peace with his

Maker by renouncing his evil ways. A large heavy Bible was raised aloft for all to see.

'The Good Book has all the answers to our problems. A pity you didn't heed its holy word earlier. An eye for an eye and all that follows.' The austere regard of the bearded man in black softened as he concluded with what he felt was a palliative to allay any trepidation that was assailing this poor sinner.

'Remember, my son, you are heading for a far, far better place after shedding this mortal coil, as indeed are we all.' Both his arms were raised to the heavens. 'Alleluia!' he called out. 'Though for us, not yet awhile,' he declared in a climactic conclusion that drew the beguiled throng into repeating the glorious declaration: 'Alleluia!'

Crado's cynical smile failed to reach his eyes as he took careful aim. The moment had arrived. The marshal stepped forward ready to slap the horse on the rump and dispatch the 'poor sinner' into the hereafter. His hand lifted.

Sweat pouring down the poor guy's wretched face was generated by the frightful uncertainty of his predicament. Continuance of life depended solely on the whim of a gringo bounty hunter whom he had known for little more than a week.

Yet here he was, suspended betwixt life and death. A no man's land, in limbo where the slightest deviation from the agreed plan could dispatch him over the edge. Into what? All he could do was prepare himself for the moment and pray, as he had never done before, that Crado Bluestone would play his part.

At that precise moment Crado fired. The bullet severed the rope just as the marshal's hand slapped the horse's rump. The prisoner's bootheels dug into his mount and the animal jumped forward. Suddenly the gloomy shroud of uncertainty was lifted, ripped off as he tore a hole in the crowd. Men leapt aside to avoid the stomping hoofs.

On the roof overlooking the action, Crado let fly with another half-dozen shells meant to keep heads down and bodies cowering. Pandemonium broke out as sheer panic gripped the crowd. Citizens stumbled hither and thither, desperate to escape the blazing attack.

Crado's face split in a suitably indulgent grin. It would be some considerable time before a posse could be raised in pursuit. The shooter didn't wait to observe the results of his spectacular performance. It was time to leave. He slithered down the steeply canting roof to the rear of the store and over the edge, landing inch perfect in the saddle of his waiting horse. The Arab stallion didn't need any urging to flee from the scene in double-quick time.

He disappeared among the huddle of buildings behind the main thoroughfare. It had been agreed that the two fugitives should meet up on the north side of Chimney Butte, the towering red sandstone rock that thrust out of the scrubland of mesquite and saguaro cacti some five miles north of Safford.

Batista arrived ten minutes before his confederate, having taken the more direct trail out of Safford. He was sprawled out on a ledge of rock gasping for breath when Crado arrived.

'Untie me quick,' he croaked out, 'and give me a drink. My throat, it is drier than the desert wind.'

Crado smirked and deliberately took his time. He dismounted and tethered his horse before slitting the bonds behind his partner's back. The water bottle was snatched from his grasp and emptied in a single draught.

'Never again,' the Mexican grunted. 'That is last time Juan Batista subjects himself to such a torment.'

That declaration soon wiped the smirk from the bounty hunter's face.

'We had a deal, pard,' he rasped, handing over a wad of well-thumbed greenbacks. 'Maybe that will help change your mind, make you see things my way.'

Seemingly indifferent to his receipt of the dough, Batista continued to berate Crado's much cherished plan for easy money.

'My whole life flashed by a hundred times waiting for that gunshot,' he wailed. 'Batista will never put himself through that again.' Then a gleam of triumph leapt across the gap separating them. 'It not work, anyway.'

'How d'you figure that out?' snapped his irritated rescuer. 'It's a perfect scheme that could be played out over and over. Easy money with no danger if'n we move about and don't choose the main towns.'

'Easy for you, maybe. Not for Batista.' He paused to light up a cigar. 'But there is one tiny problem you have not thought of.'

Crado was fuming. Somehow he managed to stifle his ire as he waited impatiently for the Mexican to reveal this mysterious flaw he had suddenly conjured up.

'So what is this vital crumb that I've overlooked?' he spat out. The sarcasm was all too obvious. He did not take kindly to having his carefully worked out strategy criticized.

Batista ignored the barbed question. His face cracked in a warped rictus. A rattler's grin would have been more friendly.

'Certainly we could pull it off one more time, maybe even two. But no more than that. The authorities are not stupid. They will soon rumble the fact that every time El Vengador is captured he is snatched from the jaws of death by a guardian angel in the guise of a hidden gunman.'

Smoke dribbled from between his pursed lips as the Mexican eyed his partner, studying his reaction. Crado turned away to hide his discomfiture. The sly varmint was right. It was something of which he had failed to take account. He gnashed his teeth in frustration. The outlaw resumed his deconstruction.

'Such things get passed around very quickly. Within two weeks, every star-packer in the territory will be on the alert . . . ' Before he had chance to pour any more cold water over the smoulder-ing ashes of Crado's plan, his hand lifted, pointing back down the trail. A plume of dust rose above the low crest of a ridge.

'It's the posse,' he called out. 'We'll branch off here and head back to the Playground through Tanque Verde Canyon. Brush out our tracks so they can't spot where we left main trail.' He turned directly to his partner. '*Rapido, hombre!* Or they will be upon us. My arms are still too stiff.'

Much as he deplored taking orders, especially from a greaser, the bounty man hurried to obey. He grabbed a dead branch of mesquite and hastily swept it across their hoof prints, backing off a short distance sufficient to avoid being noticed.

Then he spurred off after his partner around the base of Chimney Butte and into the mouth of the canyon on the far side. There they paused, waiting to see if the ploy had worked. Ten minutes later the rhythmic drumming of mounted men at the gallop grew steadily louder as the posse approached the prominent landmark.

Both men sat tense, rigid as statues, listening for a diminution of the steady throbbing. The same incessant pounding continued as the posse rode past and onward in the direction of Tucson to the west.

Crado counted ten riders. 'Looks like it fooled them,' he grudgingly acknowledged the Mexican's quick-thinking response. He had been forced to admit it to himself: that his clever subterfuge had too many holes in it to be more than a temporary expedient in the search for easy money. 'So maybe you'd better spill the beans on that claim of yours concerning a buried hoard of dough.'

'When we get back to cabin, maybe I tell.' Batista threw a chary look at his partner. 'Although last time, as I recall, you gave my offer the grand brush-off.'

'Things have changed now,' Crado replied morosely, 'as you so expressively revealed by pulling my plan apart. And I ain't gotten any others in mind.'

8

A Revolting Stash

The old abandoned cabin looked no better to Crado's jaded gaze than it had the first time he set eyes on it. Surely there had to be better places to rest up than this heap of rotten lumber. Both windows were cracked. One of the leather door-hinges had given way since they had left, allowing entry for unwelcome denizens.

Hearing their approach, a scavenging coyote slipped out through the door, carrying a skinned rabbit in its jaws.

Batista hawked out a wrathful snarl, snatched his Merlin & Hubert .44 revolver and accurately dispatched the critter to the happy hunting grounds.

'That's mighty good shooting,' Crado congratulated his partner. 'A pity we can't eat that critter. Coyote meat ain't fit for a dog. And that rabbit it stole is likely rotten by now.'

'Paah!' sneered the outlaw. 'You gringos lead an easy life. When hunger is an ever present gnawing at the belly like a bad headache, you will eat anything, even rattlesnake.' Then his manner changed abruptly. But such was the fickle nature of the guy. 'Do not worry yourself about food, *amigo*,' he assured his associate. 'Is plenty of tinned goods in cabin. El Vengador is always prepared.'

'I'm glad to hear it,' remarked Crado, tossing him a look of wary misgiving. He would do well to keep a vigilant watch on this guy. He was more unstable than a two-legged chair. 'So let's get the coffee bubbling and you can reveal all about this mysterious tale of yours.' A note of warning crept into the faintly menacing suggestion. 'And I hope for your sake it ain't going to be another piece of smooth-talking eye-wash.'

The Mexican laughed it off. 'You are

too much the cynic, Crado my friend. Place your trust in Juan Batista and you will be a winner every time.'

Crado couldn't restrain a bout of sardonic chortling at that example of homespun philosophy.

The next hour was spent clearing up the mess left by the squatting scavengers. A fresh strip of thick deer hide was nailed to the door, enabling it to the closed. By the time they had finished, the sun had set over the tranquil hideaway. Batista busied himself cooking them a meal that turned out to be amazingly tasty. Crado couldn't help noting that this guy was full of surprises. Stewed beef, pinto beans and sweet potatoes, all out of cans, was followed by pecan pie and strong coffee.

Fully replete, he went outside for a smoke. After the stuffy warmth of the cabin, the cool of evening was welcome. But only for a brief interlude. The crystal clarity of the starry sky ensured that night time in the desert was often very cold. Temperatures fell dramatically once the sun had dropped below the horizon. A stark contrast to the daytime heat that rose to furnace proportions.

The gentle rippling of the creek combined with a harmonious chirping of crickets put him in a nostalgic mood of wishful thinking. Where was Mirabelle Leguarde now? Was she still of a mind to shack up with a bounty hunter? Beauty and brains were a potent enticement for any hot-blooded dude.

Then the moment passed. He shivered. A roaring fire in the grate and that bottle of tequila sitting on the table pushed aside such wistful yearnings.

When they were both settled, glasses in hand, Crado once again broached the question of the mysterious cache.

'Believe me when I tell you that what I have to reveal is no *ensueno*,' Batista insisted. 'No idle daydream plucked out of air to gain your confidence.' A thoughtful expression softened his harsh features as the

Mexican leaned back in his chair, recollecting. Another gulp of tequila helped to focus his thoughts.

* * *

The year was 1859 in the Mexican province of Chihuahua close to the border with Texas. Hernando Batista was a simple peasant farmer, one of thousands who scraped a meagre living from the soil. Life was tough, famine an ever-present hazard in the harsh desert climate. There was little chance for relaxation. Backbreaking toil to raise crops was a never-ending fact of life.

Yet there were those at the opposite end of the social scale who made certain of their privileged position through heavy taxation. Laws were enacted by those in authority that favoured themselves over the subjugated bulk of the population. They were strictly enforced by a zealous police force supported by the military machine. The strict regime gave no thought to the welfare of its downtrodden citizens who were left to fend for themselves. It was a grim land of contrasts in which the *prominente* guaranteed themselves a life of unbridled easy and luxury.

Any attempt to try and improve the miserable lot of the peasantry was met with swift and violent resistance. Yet still dissent festered beneath the surface.

Hernando Batista was the leader of a group calling themselves the People's Freedom Movement. They met in secret with special passwords that were regularly changed to prevent infiltration by government spies. They had set out with the aim of persuading the establishment to improve their conditions through peaceful methods. But any representations made were met with hostility.

When two of Hernando's friends were hanged for their so-called effrontery, it was clear that far more ruthless and cold-blooded tactics were necessary for their claims to be taken seriously. It was abundantly clear that such tactics could only be carried out by means of forceful confrontation.

Hernando and his officers were reluctant to pursue such a drastic course. They were God-fearing men who abhorred the use of violence to solve problems. Yet they had been left with no other choice. If change was to be achieved, firm action was the only way. For that to be effective many guns would be required. Organization on military lines would be necessary.

All this would require substantial funding, and money was a commodity in short supply among the peasant population. There was only one way to secure such backing. Officials sympathetic to the Freedom Movement were able to pass on vital information to promote this cause.

An escorted carriage was leaving the provincial capital the following week to deliver the army payroll to Fort Zaragoza. There would be sufficient money on board to provide a substantial boost to the cause. Here was their chance to make a noise and force the hand of the authorities.

The ambush took place at a remote spot. Hernando and three others held up the carriage and demanded the money be handed over. There was a fierce gun battle from which only Hernando survived. He snatched the box containing the haul and fled. This was not how it was meant to be. Suddenly the full import of what he had set in motion hit the freedom fighter like an express train.

In no time the whole province was up in arms. *Federates* were called out from every station. Arrests by the score quickly followed. Whether a man was innocent or guilty, it made no difference. Brutal examples had to be made to ensure obedience to the established regime.

Hernando knew that he could not remain on his farm. Arrest would be inevitable.

Flight was his only option. But first he made sure to bury the money in a safe place. A solemn vow was made that some day he would return and make those responsible for the carnage pay the ultimate price.

'Now at last we come to the crux of the matter,' remarked Crado, having listened to the potted history of how a Mexican rebellion had been crushed. 'Where's the dough buried? That's all you need to divulge, so that we can head down there and dig it up.'

'Not so fast,' chided Baptista, wagging an admonitory finger. 'You are too impatient. Allow me to continue and you will soon see why the simple solution you propose is not possible.'

Crado resisted making a sarcastic comment, confining himself to pouring another slug of tequila into his glass. Outside an owl hooted, a triumphal sound suggesting that the predator had spotted an unwary desert rat. The listener couldn't help wishing his own search for prey could be equally straightforward. He shrugged. Nothing in this arduous life was ever that simple.

'It is good that you have taken to a proper drink. Far better than rye whiskey, eh *amigo?*' The Mexican chuckled, topping up his own glass. 'Enjoy it with this cigar.'

'Let's just get down to the mysterious bottom line,' rasped his associate. 'I knew all along that this claim of yourn was too darned good to be true.'

Batista ignored the slur as he continued with his story.

Before he left, Hernando Batista gave each of his sons a piece of paper on which was written half of a code to locate the hidden stash, which had been secreted in the largest burial ground in Chihuahua. Neither piece of paper was any use without the other: a foolproof precaution in case either of the young men was captured. Torture had frequently been used to extract information by the regime. So Hernando was taking no unwarranted risks.

Three days passed before the *federates* swept into the village of Hermaseta. Juan and his elder brother Felipe were forced to witness their home being burned to the ground. Not content with that, the heartless military trampled the crops under the stamping hoofs of their horses. The colonel in charge was all set to flog the backs off the two boys to reveal the whereabouts of Hernando Batista. Only the intervention of Rosita, their mother, stopped the brutal chastisement.

The soldiers immediately left for the frontier, hoping to catch the renegade before he reached the border formed by the Rio Grande separating Mexico from Texas. But they were too late. Hernando had already crossed into the Lone Star State. Following him was not an option. Such an act of trespass would have led to conflict with the much more powerful United States: a blatantly aggressive challenge for which the Mexican government had no stomach.

However, what they could do was hire a gunslinger to hunt down the miscreant.

It was this shock exposure of the infamous killer's name that once again brought the narration to an abrupt halt.

Monk Purvis!

Crado staggered to his feet. The glass clutched tightly in his left hand shattered. Blood mingling with the colourless spirit left him unmoved. The bounty hunter's whole being was rigid as a metal pike. His eyes bulged with the shock of hearing the name of his nemesis.

Juan Batista was likewise startled by his partner's sudden transformation. 'What is matter, Crado? What did I say to disturb you so much?'

A minute passed before the tough bounty hunter regained his self-control. 'You said that Monk Purvis went after your father. That right?'

Batista nodded. 'Felipe sent word that he had located the hired gunman and was going to challenge him. Why is he so important to you?'

Crado settled down. He needed another belt of tequila to restore his jangled nerves. Only then was he able to relate the grim events that had occurred on the Brazos and beyond all those years before.

'And I'm still chasing the varmint.' He looked at the Mexican from a fresh angle. 'Seems like we both have good reason to want that jasper in our gun sights.'

'You are right there, *amigo*. I feel it in my bones that soon we will indeed run him to ground.' Batista then made as though to resume his grim account. But Crado had one further unanswered question that had been bugging him.

'Why did you and Felipe not share your cemetery codes and unearth the loot straight away?'

'When Papa gave us each a code he made us swear on the Bible not to share the secret. Much more difficult for authorities to find stolen money if one of us was arrested. If after three months he failed to return, we were to assume he was dead. Only then were we to join forces and dig up the money to continue the rebellion in his name, but this time as guerrilla fighters.' Batista was serious about his declaration. 'You must understand that to a Mexican a promise is binding, an absolute vow. It would have been unthinkable for either of us to go against Papa's wishes.'

Six weeks later, he continued, the boys learned that Hernando had been killed by Purvis, supposedly for resisting arrest in the Texas town of Saragosa. The authorities pinned up notices all over Chihuahua boasting about their defeat of the rebel force and its leader. Felipe was incensed and strapped on his pistol. He intended seeking out Purvis and extracting his own retribution in blood. Juan wanted to accompany him, but being much younger he was persuaded to stay behind and look after their mother.

Felipe was no gunslinger and stood little chance against a seasoned killer like Monk Purvis. When his body was finally returned to the Batista family there was no sign of the paper or its all-important code.

'I can only guess that Purvis knew nothing about the hidden money when he was hired to kill Papa. The authorities will have kept that under wraps.' Batista spat in the fire. The gobbet hissed and frizzled in the flames like an angry serpent. 'It was just another job to him. Only later when Felipe called him out must he have discovered the true facts and searched the body, discovering the written-down code.'

By this time, Crado was thoroughly engrossed in this dramatic outpouring of grief and hatred. He offered his own suggestion of what had occurred next.

'So the varmint came to the right conclusion: that the code indicated where the money was buried? Only problem was, he didn't know it was only half the solution. He headed south across the border, figuring all his birthdays had come together.'

A mirthless guffaw rumbled in the Mexican's throat. 'You catch on fast, amigo. Like my good self, he must have visited the Camposanto cemetery. It is a huge place. Over a thousand graves, all in lines. A double code is essential for visitors to find the right burial places of their loved ones.'

A hearty guffaw emanated from the well-oiled bounty hunter. 'It sure must have been a sight to see him jumping around like a hornet was up his ass when he learned the truth. That I would like to have seen.'

Batista joined in the hilarity. Then his expression darkened. 'I have the other half. And I keep it up here.' He tapped his head. 'Knowing Felipe's code had been stolen, I destroyed mine. But I will never forget. It is seared upon my brain. Nor will I forget my own pledge for Monk Purvis to suffer a thousand agonies before he dies.'

'Not if'n I get to him first,' snarled Crado.

'Now you know why Juan Batista calls himself El Vengador,' the Mexican told him.

Crado nodded. Batista's story had been a startling revelation that must have been dragged from the heart. He sympathized.

Due to the bizarre circumstances that had set their lives on a parallel course, he now felt a strangely unlikely affiliation towards this Mexican bandit. It had turned out they were both seeking a similar outcome in their quest for vengeance, albeit for different reasons. There was only one fly in the ointment. Was their liaison built on stone or sand? But whatever the outcome, Crado Bluestone would be ready. Never again would he allow himself to be lulled into a false sense of security.

But he did feel some remorse for his harsh attitude towards his partner during the fake arrest in Safford. An apology was overdue. He swallowed. Such a divergence from his usual hard-bitten manner was not easy. Nevertheless, it must be done.

'Guess I ought to say sorry for giving you a tough time in Safford.' That was all. But it was enough. Crado looked away, drawing hard on the cigar.

Batista likewise dragged smoke into his lungs to consider this unexpected relaxation of the guarded mask. He accepted the brief expression of regret with a curt nod. Neither man was comfortable with outpourings of emotion. The matter was now closed. They could move on with confidence in each other's support when the crucial showdown arrived. What happened after that, only time would tell.

'The big problem is how to flush him out,' remarked Crado, settling more comfortably in his chair. 'I've been searching for the rat too darned long. And each time I get close he wriggles out of the net and disappears.'

They sat in front of the dying embers of the fire, silent and thoughtful. More tequila was drunk. At least it helped to deaden their mutual anxiety.

At last Batista announced in a low drawl: 'Perhaps there is a way to lure this fish into a net with no holes.'

9

Interlude in Tucson

Credo's curiosity had been piqued. He flicked a languid glance towards his partner. Batista puffed on his cigar before venturing to offer enlightenment.

'It all hangs on Purvis being able to read.'

Crado lifted himself from a slouch, raising his eyebrows questioningly. Noting his revived interest, the Mexican smiled as he continued:

'This gringo killer must realize by now that he needs to find the matching code if'n he is to locate the grave where Papa buried the dough.' He paused, looking keenly towards his partner for a sign of accord.

'Guess so,' drawled the still perplexed bounty hunter. 'So what's being hatched in that devious mind of yourn?'

Batista opened his mouth to reply, revealing a set of uneven yellow fangs.

'My bet is that he'll figure a relation of Felipe's is the most likely person to have it, *si?* What if we were to insert an advertisement in the personal columns of various Texas newspapers seeking information from the distraught Batista family regarding the whereabouts of their missing kin, Felipe, who disappeared some years before?'

Crado was now all ears. But he still harboured a wary scepticism. He interrupted to pose a nagging doubt.

'It's been a long spell since Felipe vanished and was gunned down. Wouldn't Purvis be leery of such a request?'

A characteristically unconcerned shrug greeted this remark. 'Sure he would. But would not any enquiry concerning the name of Felipe Batista rouse his curiosity? Anybody would be mightily intrigued, knowing there was a hefty payday at stake.'

Crado had to admit that that was a fact.

His agreement encouraged Batista to continue. 'It is most unlikely he will know that Felipe's body was returned for burial all that time ago. Hired gunmen want only their fee after making the hit. For all he knows, Felipe could have been buried in a local graveyard in Saragosa. The notice would be intended merely to locate a long-lost brother.' He seemed to shed a tear of grief which was not merely a pretence. 'For the sake of his distraught mama.'

There was much to consider once the Mexican had outlined his proposal. Both men sat awhile, mulling over the pros and cons of Batista's ingenious plan. There was much to think on. Following the breakdown of Crado's ill-conceived scheme of fake hangings, nothing could be left to chance. Monk Purvis was an experienced and highly dangerous adversary who would smell a rat a mile off.

'The newspaper appeal is a good idea.' Crado was now utterly immersed in the scheme. 'I know for sure that Purvis has learnt his letters. And he keeps up to date with local news.' He went on to explain how he had caught sight of a copy of the *Amarillo Sentinel* in the skunk's pocket. 'But it will need to be convincing.'

Over the next two days they worked hard to concoct a suitably worded notice. Finally satisfied with the result, Crado suggested he should head for the nearest large town. That was Tucson. The territorial news agency had its main office there. The editor could appraise the offering and wire it off to those journals he considered appropriate in Texas at a reasonable charge.

'When do we leave?' asked Batista, eager to get the project under way.

'Not you, pard,' cautioned Crado. 'Your ugly mug is too well-known hereabouts. I'll go in alone. Just give me a list of the supplies we'll need. Presidio

County in southwest Texas is a long ride.'

They had both reached the conclusion that Purvis was most likely to be in that neck of the woods, hoping to somehow track down the elusive stash. Maybe he even figured to strike lucky and track down the other Batista brother. If their plan succeeded this was Crado's one chance to bring his obsessive hunt to a conclusion.

The Mexican was dubious about being left behind at the cabin to twiddle his thumbs. But he soon realized that showing his well-known face in a town like Tucson would be playing with fire. A genuine hanging was not to be contemplated at this stage in the proceedings, if at all.

Crado left the next morning, assuring his partner that he would be back within the week. He placed heavy emphasis on the need for the outlaw to resist any inclination to venture out of the Devil's Playground to resume his lawless profession. The last thing Crado needed was being forced into making another rescue attempt should anything go wrong. As the outlaw himself had so eloquently pointed out, the authorities would be on their guard for just such an attempt.

Knowing that most Mexicans were staunch Catholics displaying a fervent respect for the church, Crado made Batista swear on the Bible that he would resist the temptation. With great reluctance, Batista laid a hand on the Good Book and swore a solemn oath to obey his vow of self-restraint. The deferential look that he cast towards Crado indicated that he took such a vow exceedingly seriously.

Crado could barely keep a straight face. He forcibly compressed his expression into grimly austere lines, assuming the role of a wrathful deity. The preacher in Safford had certainly impressed him. His voice rose in a crescendo of clamorous tub-thumping oratory.

'Take heed that hell and damnation will be heaped upon any person who breaks such a binding pledge. His soul will be forever cast out, forever to suffer torment in the raging fires of Hell.'

It was a wrench to bring the highly charged delivery to a close. But any further outpouring and he feared that he would burst out laughing at the terrified look upon his partner's face. But at least he was now fully satisfied that the notorious outlaw and hard man, El Vengador, would stay close to the cabin.

One detail he had omitted to confide to his unlikely partner was the prospect of his much anticipated reunion with the enchanting Mirabelle Leguarde. With any luck she would still be performing in Tucson, which was to be her next booking after Globe. Batista's presence would be a hindrance he could well do without. And there lay the possible snake in the bed.

How would she react, knowing that it was he who had freed the villain having already claimed the reward for his capture? It was a worrying question that grew ever larger, assuming seemingly insurmountable proportions the nearer he came to his destination. There was no escaping the depressing possibilities his mind conjured up. And having now hooked up with El Vengador, would that be the straw to break the camel's back?

On more than one occasion he paused. The pressing urge to turn back was almost overwhelming. Only the fact that he was almost there stayed his hand, and the fact that they did need those supplies.

After Crado had traversed the San Pedro Valley, Mount Lemmon reared up ahead. Windy Point on its south-western slopes marked the final descent to the desert floor. Tucson could be seen far below: a cluster of dirty brown and orange structures surrounded by the clutching green tentacles of giant saguaros.

The rider threaded a path down through the clumps of tamarisk, catclaw and saltbush that had managed to root in the rocky ground. Occasional red blooms of strawberry cactus and ocotillo offered a splash of brightness to the monotony of the terrain. Near the bottom of the winding narrow trail he was almost unseated by the sudden appearance of a squawking Pyrrhuloxia. The grey-and-red crested bird with its yellow parrotlike beak flew out of a crack, causing his horse to veer up on its hind legs.

'Whoa there, boy!' Crado cried out, wrestling the alarmed animal back under control. Then to the flapping flyer he smilingly chided, 'Now ain't you the careless one. Look around next time before you go upsetting innocent travellers.'

It was a light-hearted reproof that had the effect of alleviating his pessimistic mood. Yet the odd incident made Crado focus his thoughts on the stark beauty of this noble land. Desolate and austere in the extreme, but none the less offering a serenity to his troubled mind.

A man could wander for days, weeks even, without encountering a living soul. To some that would be pure torture, but to others it provided an escape, a refuge of calm. The bounty hunter sighed. It had been a strangely relaxing moment. 'A guy could sure get used to this country,' he murmured to himself. 'But how long can it survive?'

With the ever-expanding frontier pressing relentlessly westwards, in a few years the whole territory could be settled. This pristine terrain would be swallowed up by the greedy intrusion of 'civilization'. Such a fate appeared to be inevitable as more and more immigrants sought a new life in this Shangri La.

Was Crado Bluestone to be the last of his kind? Was his destiny preordained? Only time would tell. A doleful sense of his powerlessness to change things settled over him as he plodded onwards.

An hour later he had gained the flatter ground below and was cantering across the desert plain. Reality nudged aside the philosophical musings as he neared the isolated desert settlement of Tucson.

The first thing Crado noticed after passing the town's signboard was another one garishly daubed in red paint. It was impossible to ignore. That was the clear intention. Visitors were firmly warned that they were now entering a gun-free zone. All newcomers were required to hand in their weapons at the sheriff's office. They could be collected when their owners left town.

This particular newcomer's eyes lifted. The decree was one of those infrequent instances when it became necessary to have his US deputy marshal's badge on display. When so doing he could legitimately retain his firearms. He slowly guided the black stallion down the centre of the main street. It was soon obvious that the local lawdog was no slouch in ensuring that his orders were obeyed. No guns were on display.

Crado nodded his approval. Then his eye caught sight of a notice that he had been expecting. *Wanted — Dead or Alive! The notorious outlaw and killer known as El Vengador.* The price on his new partner's head had risen to 3,000 bucks. Crado whistled. The thought fizzed through his head that perhaps he ought to have stuck with his known profession. Just as quickly he discarded it.

If nothing else, he regarded himself as an honourable man. Treachery and playing the Judas hand did not sit well on his broad shoulders. Anyway, the money Batista claimed was awaiting them at Camposanto far outweighed such a paltry sum. But most important of all was the chance being offered to run up against Monk Purvis.

As he spotted the Palace Theatre on the far side of the main drag, his thoughts shifted again to Mirabelle Leguarde. Did he still have a future with her?

The lady in question was at that very moment on stage. A matinée performance had been added to the scheduled programme on account of the singer's popularity. Performing here in Tucson was a prestigious step up for the artiste who was hoping that a legitimate agent would be on hand to further her career.

Much as her stated affection for the bounty hunter, Crado Bluestone, had been genuine at the time, now she recognized that it had been too recklessly declared. Spontaneity was all right when buying clothes or a new hat, but where affairs of the heart were concerned far more circumspection was required. Crado had stated as much himself, for which in hindsight she was extremely relieved.

As he had queried, was she yet ready for the humdrum routine of everyday life outside the spotlight? In truth she thought not. At least not yet. Maybe when her popularity began to fade it would be a different matter. All these and other matters had been tossed over in her head during the days following her paramour's departure. It did not help his cause when she discovered his part in the blatant chicanery played out to rescue of the fraudulent outlaw.

Notwithstanding all these considerations, upon her catching sight of this man at the back of the theatre her stomach was sent aflutter, along with a trembling of her vocal chords. He still had that effect. The nervous reaction was quickly overcome: only another performer of equal skill would have noticed the wobbly notes.

Her superlative presentation was brought to its conclusion earlier than expected. Grumbles were easily silenced when the singer made a special promise.

'I'm sorry for the early curtain-call, boys.' She held up her hands, instantly quieting the disgruntled murmurs down. 'But don't worry. As a special treat, you're all cordially invited to the evening performance at no extra charge.'

Cheers erupted from the whole gathering as Mirabelle bowed low before making her exit. She badly needed to compose her thoughts in private. This man had played her false by his actions. In that respect he was no better than the skunk he had rescued. He would need to eat a great deal of humble pie to gain her forgiveness.

Hearing the girl's dulcet tones once again brought a lump to the newcomer's throat. He felt like a right heel. Once she had left the stage Crado shouldered his way through the crowd over to the bar. He needed a cold drink to slake a dry throat after his long trek, not to mention time for reflection on how best to approach the girl. All his thoughts were on the knotty dilemma of how to counter her resentment of his shameful conduct.

In this state of mind he failed to notice another man at the end of the bar, whose scowl of recognition had not passed unnoticed by those in his immediate vicinity. The husky growl of anger deep within the guy's throat implied that trouble was about to erupt. Rowdy Slag Bassett levered himself off the bar. A Brooklyn Slocum .32 pocket pistol appeared in his hand. Easy to conceal, it had served Bassett well in the past to get the drop on his victims.

Men quickly sought to remove themselves from the line of fire. The two adversaries were left alone at the bar. Yet still Crado remained unaware of the danger, now only a hair's-breadth away. The pistol rose to deliver its small but lethal bullet. Crado raised his second glass of beer.

He was just about to take a gulp when a warning cry cut through the highly charged atmosphere. It came from the veranda at the rear of the theatre.

'Crado! Crado! Behind you, he's got a gun!'

Mirabelle had been slowly descending the stairs intent on making her feelings clear. From her elevated position she commanded a perfect view of everything that was taking place in the auditorium below. The danger posed by Bassett was easily spotted. Her shrieking reaction was instinctive.

Five years of successfully evading backshooters, bushwhackers and tricksters of every description now kicked in. Crado dropped like a stone to the floor as the deadly chunk of lead scored a furrow across his scalp. It was no more than a graze and did little damage but nonetheless the bullet had felt like a branding-iron, searing and hot.

He palmed his own gun as he rolled over to face his assailant. Only when the hogleg spat flame did Crado recognize the sullen face of Rowdy Slag Bassett. The jasper was clearly still seething over his besting in the tussle over El Vengador.

The heavier .44 slug struck the aggrieved man in the left shoulder, spinning him around. Bassett was right-handed and so still posed a dangerous risk to life and limb. He clung on to the bar, trying to trigger off a second shot. But the wound had slowed him down.

Crado didn't give him a second chance. He emptied the Colt revolver, then drew the Schofield ready to finish the job. It was not necessary. Slag Bassett was splayed out across a card table, looking like a red colander. Now, with the fracas brought to a sudden and violent conclusion, men appeared from cover. Only one topic stood out amid the animated buzz of conversation. It wasn't the recent rise in the cost of whiskey.

Strong yet gentle arms hauled Crado to his feet.

'That head wound needs treating. Come with me quickly.' The wounded man turned, allowing Mirabelle to lead him away. But he suddenly felt light-headed. They had reached the bottom of the stairs when another more abrasive voice called out.

'Hold it right there, mister.' It was Sheriff Bart Maston. He was holding a double-barrelled twelve-gauge, evidently with the purpose of using it if necessary. 'You're under arrest for carrying firearms within the town limits. And I'll add a charge of disturbing the peace as well. Maybe even murder.' A leery smirk creased the lawman's face. 'Now drop them irons and raise your hands. This Loomis will take your head clean off at this range, and likely your saviour's as well. I ain't too fussed about your health. But I'd sure hate to be the cause of terminating this lady's career.' The shotgun wagged. 'It's your call.'

'This man was only defending himself,' the singer protested. 'He would have been gunned down by that backshooter if I hadn't shouted a warning.' She assumed her most alluring smile before adding, 'And there's a room full of witnesses here to back me up.'

'And I'm a deputy US marshal, Sheriff,' Crado interjected, tapping the badge pinned to his vest, 'which permits the holder to bear arms at all times.'

Bart Maston scowled. He was not accustomed to having his authority challenged by any newcomer just arrived in Tucson. This was his town. He was the law here. And he had every intention of making darned sure this turkey knew it.

Shoulders squared off, the lawman's bristling black moustache twitched with irritation. He took a couple of steps forward, forcing the silenced crowd to back off. The shotgun was now joined by a brutal revolver with a twelve-inch barrel known as a Buntline Special. The sheriff was not for backing down. He meant business.

'A man's been killed, fella. And you're a stranger in town. Until I get to the bottom of what's happened here and check out those credentials, you can be my guest over at the hoosegow. Now shift your ass!'

'You can't treat him like this,' Mirabelle persisted firmly. 'Can he

162

folks?' Her fervent appeal was meant to gain support from the milling throng. But they all remained silent to a man. Nobody was going to interfere with Sheriff Maston, the guy who had single-handedly tamed the wildest town in the south-west. His rigid, obdurate adherence to the letter of the law had led to him being labelled Iron Bart. It fitted him like a glove.

Crado shrugged his shoulders. There was no arguing with a twelve-gauge and a Buntline.

'Guess I ain't got much choice, then.' He sighed. Then, offering his lady-love a bashful smile, he said:. 'But much obliged to you for saving my life. I owe you for that. Let's hope I can get this guy to see sense.'

But there was no chance of that. What Iron Bart Maston failed to reveal was that he held a long-standing grudge against the renowned bounty hunter. The two men had never met. But Crado's name was well-known in legal circles. Maston had attempted to follow a similar trail some years previously. But he had only ever been a novice in comparison.

Crado had beaten him to the punch on three separate occasions when they were both tracking the same wanted men. Realizing he was not cut out for such a highly lucrative though precarious life, Maston had opted for the less well-paid, steadier job of administering the law on an official basis.

Crado Bluestone falling into his lap offered the chance to get even that he relished.

Having been dumped in the town's smelly cellblock, Crado lay down on the hard bunk bed. In Tucson for less than an hour, and here he was, incarcerated by a bellicose loud-mouthed starpacker for defending himself. He hadn't even been given the opportunity to visit the local newspaper office.

To add insult to injury, his head felt like a mule had stamped on it.

10

Changing Places

One week had passed since Crado left the hideout in the Devil's Playground. Juan Batista expected the return of his partner any day now. Then they could put their plan into operation. More days passed. But after two weeks there was still no sign of the missing bounty hunter. Batista was becoming distinctly ill at ease.

Stamping around the cabin, he vehemently berated himself for agreeing to let the gringo travel to Tucson alone. Why had he not returned? Had something gone wrong? But what? Crado Bluestone was not on the wanted lists. He was of the kind who went after villains with a price on their heads.

All manner of bizarre reasons floated

round in the Mexican's head as he desperately tried to figure out what had happened. Had the man-hunter betrayed El Vengador and was now seeking to claim the reward for his capture? But that did not ring true. A posse would have been here by now if such was his intention.

No further theories were forthcoming. So what should he do now? Go it alone? He could place the advertisement himself and head down to Saragosa in Texas. Hesitation rippled across the crumpled leather of his face. That was no solution. Monk Purvis could only be given the finger by Crado. And there was another problem. Going up against such a cunning adversary on his ownsome was too risky.

Then an emotional tug, long since confined to the annals of his past, hardened his features once more, brought about by a soupçon of concern for his partner's welfare, vying for attention with the need to retrieve the graveyard's hidden secret.

The former concern was a deeply unsettling phenomenon that Batista was loath to acknowledge. He tried shrugging it off as of no consequence. Emotional sentiments should be reserved for family alone, certainly not wasted on hard-bitten gun-toters. But the feeling remained. Crado was in trouble; he felt it in his bones. So Juan Batista had to assume the unaccustomed role of his brother's keeper.

Once the decision had been made, he wasted no time in setting off to help his amigo. 'Amigo!' Batista repeated the word aloud. This time it carried a far more poignant resonance. 'Amigo!' Did he actually mean it? The poser was dismissed as more pragmatic issues came forward.

Eventually the Mexican found himself in the very same position as Crado had been in weeks before, when he had first reached the Tucson town limits. He tugged the Texas sombrero down over his eyes to conceal the contours of a face splashed across numerous Wanted dodgers. No sense in advertising his arrival to any gun-happy jigger eager to make a name for himself. Although, on spotting the poster pinned up on a wall, he couldn't help cracking a satisfied smirk of pride. To be worth 3,000 US dollars was no mean achievement.

He drew his horse into the side of the main street outside a saloon and sat for a while, pondering over how to proceed from here. Should he just walk into the nearest saloon and make enquiries? That was a solution fraught with hazard. He could easily be recognized. If Crado had gotten himself in some deep shit, anybody asking about him could end up in the same mire. But something had to be done.

The problem was solved by the unexpected appearance of Mirabelle Leguarde sashaying down the board-walk towards him. So this was why Crado had insisted his new partner remain at the cabin. Batista smiled to himself. The guy clearly didn't want any unwelcome competition. He placed himself directly in her path, forcing the girl to pull up. Removing his sombrero, he bowed to her with a debonair flourish.

'So, we meet again, *señorita*,' he declared. 'Perhaps you have knowledge concerning the whereabouts of our mutual acquaintance, Senor Crado Bluestone?'

Momentarily caught on the wrong foot, Mirabelle was lost for words. El Vengador was the last person she expected to encounter on Tucson's main thoroughfare. Her parasol slipped from nerveless fingers. Still electing to play the suave dandy, Batista retrieved it.

That was when she reacted. The unctuous smile, that sycophantic wheedling, all the traits she had come to despise in this odious creature caused the old disgust to well up inside her. All her pent-up frustrations at this man's effrontery were brought to bear as she lashed Batista across the head.

Once, twice, the parasol struck home before the victim was able to grab the weapon and wrench it free of her hands. Luckily, nobody had witnessed the assault, and the blows had not caused any damage, except perhaps to the victim's pride. He quickly pulled her into an alleyway to ensure that that remained the case.

'Why you attack Batista so?' he complained, rubbing a sore head. 'What I do to deserve such treatment?'

The girl was fuming. 'You have the nerve to stand there and deny you cheated me out of good money with your lying fancy words.' Once again she attempted to strike the Mexican. But he held her fast.

'A misunderstanding, *señorita*,' he pleaded, 'and if you thought otherwise, then I sincerely apologize for any inconvenience to your good self.' Another bow followed as he released her. But he made a point of stepping back to avoid any further injury.

'Save it, buster,' she replied waspishly

having regained her poise. 'I don't believe a word of your cheap smooth-talking flattery. You're nothing but a sneaky rat, a scheming no-account — '

Batista held up a hand, cutting short the girl's derision with an insolent smile. Such insults were like water off a duck's back to him. It was time to get down to business.

'Enough of this *parloteo, señorita*,' he chided. 'Do not bother to deny that Crado Bluestone came here seeking you out. He is in hiding around here. And you know where. Has he not told you that we are partners in a most rewarding venture?'

The girl broke down. Tears welled in her eyes. Batista regretted his brisk tone and forthright attitude. He put an arm around her shoulder to offer some comfort. But she took it the wrong way and brushed his gesture aside.

'Yes, he told me all about your shady agreement,' she snapped back, dabbing a handkerchief to her eyes. 'And now he's stuck in jail. I visit him every day.

For some reason Sheriff Maston has it in for him. He doesn't believe that Crado is innocent of any crime. That man he shot and killed was trying to ambush him . . . '

Batista eyes widened with shock. He held up a hand to stem her flow of words.

'Perhaps we should retire somewhere more appropriate and you can tell me the whole story,' he suggested. 'I came here when he did not return to our hideout. Never did I imagine he could have landed himself in such hot water.'

Once the pair of unlikely allies were ensconced in Mirabelle's lodgings, she related all that had happened in the Palace Theatre that fateful day, now almost three weeks past. When she had finished both of them fell silent, considering the implications of her eye-opening account.

'Rowdy Slag Bassett leaving this world is no great loss,' he said with a snigger, remembering the critter's failed attempt to gun him down. 'Dry-gulching an adversary is what I would expect from such a charlatan.' He conveniently chose to ignore his own discourteous treatment of Mirabelle. 'So when is the circuit judge due to arrive? Because he will surely have to order a release once the true facts are related in court.'

'Not for another six weeks at least,' sobbed the girl, dabbing her watery eyes. 'Meanwhile he has to languish in that stinking hole.'

It was clear to Batista that the girl was smitten with his partner. But a more pressing concern was how to release Crado from jail. Hanging around Tucson for all that time was out of the question, Each day he remained in the town, his chances of being identified increased substantially.

The only option was to break Crado out of jail. He stroked a bristly chin, his devious brain deep in thought. The problem now was to figure out a way that would enable them both to escape back into the Devil's Playground. Mirabelle was in agreement, provided no harm came to the prisoner.

★ ★ ★

While the singer was engaged in her evening performance Batista put all his guile and cunning into devising a plan of action. She had allowed him stay in her room provided he remained absolutely quiet. Her starchy landlady was adamant that no male visitors were allowed to remain on the premises after dark. It was not until the early hours of the following morning that he eventually arrived at a suitable modus operandi. The key to its successful accomplishment lay with Mirabelle Leguarde.

When she eventually returned to the lodging house Batista presented the scheme he had in mind.

'Does the sheriff search you during each visit to the jail?' he asked.

Mirabelle snorted with indignation.

'That's the part the turkey enjoys most of all. And I have no option but to endure his lecherous pawing.'

'What about anything you take in for the prisoner? Is that searched?'

'I always take in his meals,' she replied, wrathfully tossing her long tresses of raven hair. 'The slop they serve up is only fit for the pigs. But he doesn't bother with that. It's me that his debauched gaze is fixed upon.'

Batista couldn't rightly blame the guy for that. She sure was a *bella chica*. He forced his thoughts back to the task in hand.

'That is the weakness we will exploit.' He went on to explain that inside a bowl supposedly containing a pie there would be an iron crowbar with which to chip away at the cement securing the cell bars. As luck would have it, the window faced on to a back yard. 'It should take him no more than two days to loosen enough cement for my horse to then drag the bars free. But he'll have to be careful not to make a lot of noise. Think you can manage that?'

'It is a good plan, but it will put me under suspicion once he has escaped,' the girl agreed doubtfully. 'Maston is no fool. He'll know it was me who supplied the crowbar.'

'Then you will have to come with us. Though that will make you a fugitive as well.' Batista was sympathetic and offered the girl the chance to turn down his suggestion, but added, 'There is no other way, Mirabelle. It is all or nothing.'

He waited on tenterhooks while she tossed over the stark implications of what she was about to become embroiled in. Was it worth giving up a burgeoning career for a man she barely knew? Once the plan was set in motion, there could be no going back. Yet when it came down to the wire, there was no choice. She was enamoured of this man, and love knew no boundaries.

A cool detachment accompanied her brisk nod of acceptance. Her whole body went rigid as she braced herself for the coming ordeal. Batista laid a reassuring hand on her trembling shoulder. This time she did not flinch. They were all partners in crime now. Even though it was being forced on to them by a belligerent lawman.

A strange calmness suffused the girl's whole body. A decision had been made and she knew it was the right one.

The key element of the plan to release the prisoner lay in providing a distraction that would draw the sheriff and his deputies away from the jailhouse. Only then could Batista move into the rear compound, which would normally be under surveillance.

'I could start a fire at the back of the theatre,' suggested Mirabelle. 'In the early hours when everyone is asleep, a fire in one of the empty buildings where they store all the props is the obvious choice. No one would be put at risk. And it would take some time before it was noticed and the alarm was raised. That would allow me time to get out of town.'

Batista nodded his approval. 'It is a good plan.' This girl had a sharp brain as well as iridescent beauty. 'I passed an old adobe mission on the eastern edge of town. We will meet up there. The darkness will hide our escape back to the Devil's Playground.'

So it was arranged. Crado was to be apprised of the plan the following day. All being well, they could put it into operation a couple of days after that. In the meantime, Batista would need to check out the back of the jail under cover of darkness. He could not afford to be spotted.

Nor could he remain in the lodging house. Mirabelle suggested he hide out in the theatre's prop shed during daylight hours. It was only visited at the start of a fresh performance when new stage scenery was set up. She could supply him with regular meals.

'It will only be for a couple of days. After dark, you can emerge and get acquainted with the town's layout,' she told him.

A sly glint appeared in the Mexican's shifty gaze as he said, 'Don't forget to include a bottle of Scotch whisky.' He hurried to address the sour grimace with which she greeted this request. 'Only to keep out the night time chill, you understand.'

The next couple of days were sheer misery to a man of Juan Batista's disposition. During the daylight hours he felt like a prisoner himself. After what seemed like a bagful of sunsets, the night arrived for the breakout. It was a first for the Mexican. Although he was nervous at the prospect, it was also exhilarating.

11

Breakout

Once he had been told of the plan to break him out of the jailhouse Crado used every available second to dig away at the adobe cement securing the cell bars. Luckily it was an old building and the mortar had never been replaced. Much of it crumbled when he dug in the iron rasp. Not knowing when the deputies would check up on him was draining on his nerves. On more than one occasion he was forced to make excuses for the unusual scraping noises emanating from the block.

'What the heck you doing in there, Bluestone?' snapped a mean-faced deputy called Sadeye Jones, who came bustling into the cellblock. His drooping peepers scanned the cell for signs of illicit activity. But Crado was already lying on his bunk, nonchalantly puffing on a stogie.

'Just a hungry mouse that took a fancy to that tasty grub you guys dole out. I soon sent him packing.' This sarcastic sally was lost on Jones, who merely grunted before returning to the front office and a lurid dime novel he was reading.

Crado sniggered at the retreating back. Neither Maston nor his underlings ever suspected that skulduggery was afoot. As soon as the coast was clear, he resumed the steady task of loosening the cell bars.

On the night chosen for the break Crado had to force himself to act normally. Inside his guts were churning over. He was sweating, his nerve-ends tingling. How the custodians didn't notice he could not imagine. Perhaps the idea of anyone escaping from imprisonment had never occurred to them.

At the appointed hour a low muttering in the office suddenly grew into frenzied shouting. The words *fire* and *spreading* brought a wicked grin to his unshaven countenance. Mirabelle had clearly played her part. The conflagration had been sighted. Panic-stricken orders were followed by sounds of slamming doors as his jailers departed to investigate.

All Crado could hope for now was that the girl had made good her own escape and was waiting behind the mission on the edge of town.

Moments later he heard the expected call from outside in the yard: a muted owl hoot. Batista must be in place. The night sky was almost as black as coal. A thin quarter-moon overhead gave insufficient light to hamper the escape. Batista had brought his own horse round to the rear of the jail where Crado's black stallion was conveniently tethered. He slunk into the yard and over to the barred window.

'Are you ready, *amigo?*' he hissed. A grunted response was all that was needed. He tossed the end of a lariat through the bars. 'Fasten this tightly round the bars, then stand back.'

Out front, fear-induced shouting and hollering was all aimed at the burgeoning blaze. In the arid regions of the West, fire was one of the most dreaded of hazards. With most buildings constructed of wood, whole towns could be reduced to ashes in the blink of an eye. Already a dull glow indicated that this one had taken a substantial hold of the storage shed's dry timbers.

The structure was isolated from other nearby buildings, so containing the blaze within it should be simple. None of the participants in the clandestine venture had any wish to be a party to wholesale destruction.

The other end of the rope was tied round the saddle horn. Batista mounted up and walked the mustang forward until the rope tightened. Then he vigorously applied the spur rowels, urging the cayuse to pull hard.

'Come, my beauty!' he muttered in the horse's ear, trying to keep the anxiety from his voice. 'Pull, pull with all your might.'

Muscles straining to their limits, the hardy animal laboured to shift the reluctant obstacles to freedom. But the bars held firm. Only a smattering of dust and a few pebbles fell away. Sweat coated the Mexican's face as he vehemently exhorted the horse to greater efforts.

Inside the cell, Crado knew that insufficient mortar had been dug away. He dragged his bunk away from the wall. It was heavy, but sheer panic at what failure would mean lent extra strength to his exertions. Raising the cumbersome frame, he slammed it against the loosened section of wall. Once, twice, three times.

Then suddenly the stubborn adobe cracked. A deep fissure appeared in the rock-hard adobe wall as if it had been struck by a lightning flash. It surrendered to the battering ram. The cell bars disappeared along with bricks and rubble, leaving a rough-edged hole.

The fugitive wasted no further time: he scrambled through the gap. Any minute now the alarm could be raised. He dashed over to where Batista was holding his horse and leapt into the saddle.

Without uttering a word both men spurred off, twisting and turning between the shadowy outlines of back lots previously reconnoitred by the Mexican. Behind them, flames from the blazing shed were clearly visible against the blackness of the night sky. But no gunshots pursued the fugitives.

'Is good, eh Crado, *mi amigo?*' Batista's teeth gleamed white in a savage smile of triumph, 'Is not Juan Batista a clever *hombre* to have planned such a perfect job?'

Crado's concern was more for the safety of Mirabelle than bolstering his partner's self-esteem. Already they were nearing the old Catholic mission. Would she be there to greet them? He was on tenterhooks as his straining vision probed the blurred outline of the meeting place. Heart in mouth, he searched desperately for signs of movement.

Then she emerged from behind a wall. Crado leapt off his horse and hurried across. She threw herself into his arms. Tears of joy thrust aside any concerns of what the future might hold. The sheer exultation of successfully orchestrating a jail-break of the man she loved overrode all else.

They kissed. Her lips yielded to his touch. For a moment the reality of their situation melted away. A nirvana of their very own wrapped itself around the entwined bodies. On this occasion there were no reservations expressed. Indeed no words were needed as the world stood still. But it was only a fleeting moment.

'Come!' urged Batista. 'We must go. Soon they will discover the truth and be on our tail.'

So it was back to earth with a bump. No sooner was the warning uttered than a horrified shout rang out above the general hubbub of alarm.

'Hey Sheriff! The prisoner's escaped!'

The fugitives mounted up and quickly disappeared into the early morning haze.

★   ★   ★

The day after reaching the cabin hidden deep within the labyrinth of the Devil's Playground, the trio of fugitives left in pursuit of their quest. The first item on their agenda was to have the missing-person's notice publicized in newspapers across Texas. But then the most pressing need was to get out of Arizona. Wanted posters would soon be posted across the territory for three fugitives. With one being a woman, the trio would be easy to recognize.

Consequently they had to avoid all the main towns. Only when they had crossed the border into New Mexico were they able to relax. After descending the Buckhorn Trail through the

Mogollon Mountains the first settlement they reached was Silver City. It was a rough-and-ready town, primarily devoted to hard-rock mining. No awkward questions were likely to be asked here.

Crado was concerned that Mirabelle should not be dragged into the showdown that was inevitable should their scheme of flushing out Monk Purvis succeed. After due deliberation it was agreed between the pair of starry-eyed paramours that this was the best place for her to remain until it was all over.

They booked rooms at the National Hotel. After Mirabelle had departed to seek work, the two conspirators settled down to construct an appropriate notice to entice the Jack o' Lantern out of hiding. It was vital that their message be honed to ensure the most impact. The final epistle was brief with a snappy heading aimed to attract the attention of the right person. It read:

HAVE YOU SEEN FELIPE
BATISTA?
Anyone who has knowledge of the
whereabouts of Felipe Batista
should come to Saragosa in Texas
and make himself known to his
long-lost brother Juan. He is the
elder son of Hernando and Rosita,
late of Hermaseta in Chihuahua
Province, Mexico. A reward is
offered for any information leading
to Felipe's reunion with his distraught family.
Signed: Juan Batista

With the message written out, they
wandered out on to the street. A short
stroll along the busy boardwalk brought
them to the local law office. An
instinctive reaction from the bounty
hunter was to study the pinned up
notices for any worthwhile Wanted
dodgers. Crado and his partner were
relieved to find that none were on
display seeking their arrest.

'Looks like we're in the clear in New

189

Mexico, buddy,' remarked Crado.

Only one dodger was pinned up. A young hot-shot going by the name of Billy the Kid had been arrested for larceny. He had subsequently escaped from the town jail by climbing up a chimney. Real name Henry Antrim, the Kid had then fled over the rooftops and 'disappeared among the willows, gone on the scout'.

That described the beginning of a criminal career that was to have repercussions way beyond the limits of Silver City.

'Looks like the Kid has made a right fool of the dudes running this berg.' Crado couldn't resist a hearty chuckle.

Batista was caught up in the bout of laughter. 'I think we are going to hear a lot more of this *hombre* in the near future,' he agreed. 'And it says here that the jail is only six months old and meant to be escape proof.'

The incident caused both men much hilarity. Hearing the outburst of laughter on the street, the marshal stomped out of his office. His grim scowl hinted that he was not amused by their scoffing guffaws at his expense.

'What's all the ruckus? You critters looking for trouble?' he rapped out. 'We don't take kindly to no-account drifters stopping in our town.'

Contrite expressions immediately replaced the mocking grins. 'All we want is to find the newspaper office, Marshal,' burbled Crado, affecting his most humble and contrite demeanour. 'We need to place an advert. Then we'll be out of here pronto.'

Batista clutched his sombrero, nodding. 'Is so, *señor*, we are simple cowboys, looking for work.'

The sheepish expressions worked wonders with the pompous official. Applejack Biff Nichols puffed up his shoulders. His rotund belly wobbled. A penchant for the fruity desserts had landed him with the less than flattering nickname, though it was never spoken to his face. The lawman might not look the part of a tough town-tamer, but that was exactly what he had been in his youth. Folks in Grant County still talked about his besting of the Stillwell Gang back in '61.

'Glad to hear it,' he scoffed. 'Malingerers ain't welcome in Silver City. The *Herald* office is two blocks west on the far side.' A casually waved thumb indicated the direction. Sniffing down his bulbous snout, the lawdog then hitched up his gunbelt and sauntered over to the Wishing Well saloon for his twice-daily libation.

Both men breathed sighs of relief. Batista wiped the beads of sweat bubbling on his brow.

'Phew! That was a close call, *amigo*,' he murmured. 'We do not want to take Billy's place. I expect after his unwelcome breakout they have blocked up the offending chimney.'

The last thing they needed at this stage in their plans was to attract unwanted attention from nosy starpackers. They hurried off down the street stifling another fit of the giggles. The editor of the *Silver City Herald* kept them waiting for half an hour while he repaired the printing press. The paper was a one-man operation. It was clear that an assistant was needed if the guy was not to have a heart attack.

'Sorry for the delay, gents,' he spluttered, dragging an ink-stained rag across his face once he got round to seeing them, 'But as you see, I'm kept kinda busy.'

After hearing their request, the editor raised no objections to the personal advert being distributed throughout the territory and beyond into West Texas. The harassed man promised to send the wire off to his contacts once the latest edition of the *Herald* had been prepared.

'Sorry, but there ain't no chance of that for at least three days,' Clark Brooker apologized with a lift of his hands. 'I'm in the middle of printing the latest edition of the *Herald*. That takes priority over everything else.' He grunted, jabbing an admonitory thumb at the obstinate printer. 'And as you can see, I've got problems with the darned equipment. Only when that's fixed and the print run is completed can I sort out your business.'

Appeals regarding the importance of their mission were met with regretful but firm rebuttals. He would not be moved. It was only when Crado slipped a substantial extra payment into Brooker's hand that the editor's stubborn attitude miraculously changed. His beady eyes popped behind the pebble-lensed spectacles. That sort of dough could buy him a new printer.

Accordingly, his assurance was instantly forthcoming that he would send off the notice that very same day.

'Rest assured, gents,' he breezed, stuffing the dough into his jeans before these dudes could change their minds. 'I'll include definite stipulations regarding the urgency of the matter. I have numerous contacts throughout the south-west. So with my backing, there'll be no delays. You can be certain of that.'

'We're much obliged for your enthusiastic cooperation,' Crado enthused sardonically, curling his lips in a sarcastic smile. But the editor was not listening. His mind was fixed upon the model of printer he intended to purchase.

The duo left the newspaper office more than satisfied with the outcome of their visit. It called for a celebratory drink. But not at the Wishing Well. They had no desire to encounter Applejack Nichols.

★　★　★

They spent a couple of days resting up and replenishing their meagre supplies. The leave-taking between Crado and his new love was painful, but both parties knew it was essential. No distractions could be afforded if the culprit was to be lured out of hiding. After asking around, Mirabelle had been offered work as a singer in the Golden Nugget saloon. It wasn't the

Palace in Tucson, but it would suffice.

This was the one time in his life when Crado was reluctant to press on into the unknown. The only consolation was that it was merely a temporary separation. Once the dual task of ridding the world of Monk Purvis and securing a grubstake for the future had been completed, he would return to Silver City to claim the most alluring prize of all. That thought kept him going as the two partners headed south-east in pursuit of their quarry.

12

Web of Deceit

From Silver City they headed east, crossing the Cookes Range where a strange rock formation smote their eyes. It was like a city of boulders standing isolated in the middle of a sandy wilderness. A bent neck of grey stone appropriately called Dinosaur Rock lorded it over the other sentinel rocks. Crado was fascinated. Batista, however, was more concerned about avoiding the Apaches, led by their warrior chief Cochise who regarded this as his land.

The constant need to watch for any movement on the horizon made both men edgy. So it was with a great deal of relief that they espied the old Mexican town of Mesilla. From there it was but a short ride south to the border town of

El Paso. Now it was time to check whether editor Clark Brooker had kept his word. Both men avidly perused a copy of the *El Paso Courier* over a couple of cold beers in the Border saloon.

Heart in mouth Crado scanned each page, becoming ever more tense as they revealed nothing of interest. Batista was fluent in gringo speech, but of the written word he was ignorant.

'Is there nothing?' he railed as each unrewarding page was turned. 'That cheating news dog will answer to Juan Batista for his treachery.'

Crado struggled to prevent himself uttering an acid rejoinder, although he was beginning to feel the same way. Then he saw it. There on the very last page along with all the other personal announcements.

It had indeed been given a prominent position in thick heavy type that nobody could ignore. The two men's sense of relief was palpable. They ordered more drinks as they studied the notice in its entirety. If Monk Purvis was in the vicinity of Saragosa, three days' ride to the south-east, he could not fail to notice it. The name of Felipe Batista had even been emphasized.

'You guys look like you've won the monthly lottery,' the bartender commented after noticing their upbeat demeanour.

Crado responded with a wry smirk. 'You could say that we've certainly learned something to our advantage,' he replied, quickly assuming a bland expression that gave nothing away.

The barman raised his eyebrows, hoping for more details. He was to be disappointed. The two men left soon after, eager to continue their journey.

'You think Purvis will be in Saragosa by now?' Batista enquired of his partner.

Crado gave the query some thought before offering his opinion. 'It all hinges on the skunk still being in West Texas, and being within easy reach if'n he's read the advert. We've been making a heap of assumptions regarding the guy's movements. All we can do is trust that our figuring was on the mark.'

They were suddenly faced with a shedful of imponderables, random speculations that might or might not turn up trumps. Why should Monk Purvis be anywhere close by? He could easily have headed north to Colorado or even up into Canada. It was a downcast pair of treasure-seekers who plodded across the open-range country.

Now that they were almost within reach of the jackpot, luck was showing its fickle nature. The call had been made, the cards laid down face up. All they could hope for was that their reckoning had given them a winning-hand. More to the point: that the four-flusher had not smelt a set-up being prepared.

After leaving El Paso they soon passed the Socorro Mission, after which the trail faded into a sun-baked wilderness. The undulating acres of the Hudspeth Sink stretched away as far as the eye could see, and beyond as well. It was a bleak prospect. They could now see that the recommendation from the livery barn ostler to take a pack mule had been no idle scaremongering. This was one serious piece of real estate that demanded respect if a safe passage was to be ensured.

Five days later and with a great sense of relief they eventually came out on the other side. Dust-caked and with their water supply down to the final drops, the tormenting mirage of a cold beer could now be turned into a thirst-quenching reality.

Saragosa was just another shabby huddle of adobe structures, but at least it had a hotel and cantina. The two men pointed their horses to the former.

Crado was unfamiliar with this part of Texas, unlike Batista who had sad memories of when he accompanied his mother to collect Felipe's bullet-riddled corpse. The Mexican struggled to hide the conflicting sentiments churning away at his guts, but pride forbade any outward display of emotion. A granite-hard exterior did not fool his partner but Crado said nothing.

Booking in at the Salt Draw Hotel elicited the information that they were the only current guests. A tentative enquiry of the guy behind the desk, asking if anybody had been looking for a certain Juan Batista, produced only a shake of the head.

Harper Smith adjusted his spectacles then turned the visitors' book around.

'Welcome to Saragosa, Mr Smith and Mr Brown. I hope you enjoy your stay with us.' It had been agreed between both partners beforehand that they should assume false names. No sense in advertising their presence. The element of surprise was vital if Purvis were to be caught on the hop.

Not even a flicker of disbelief cracked the bewigged proprietor's deadpan expression. All manner of disparate individuals passed through the town. What his guests chose to call them-selves was their business. So long as they paid up on time and caused no trouble, he couldn't have cared less.

'You look all in, *amigo*,' Batista said as they trudged up the stairs to their room. 'What you need is a good rest.'

'Can't disagree with you there, pard,' replied Crado, stifling a yawn. 'Reckon I'm getting a mite too old for this kind of life. Chasing after desperadoes on the prod and always looking over your shoulder in case some jasper with a grudge decides to take you down is a young fella's call. After this job I'm calling it a day.'

The bed in their room looked mighty comfortable. After dragging off his hat and coat Crado flopped down. As his eyes closed, visions of the delectable Mirabelle Leguarde brought a smile to his drowsy features.

'You have sleep while I take a stroll around and get the lie of the land,' murmured Batista. 'It is some time since I was last in Saragosa. Things can change quickly.' Even before the Mexican had finished speaking, his *compadre* was dead to the world. The steady rumble of snoring brought a sly grin to Batista's face. He quietly closed the door and left to visit the Diablo Cantina on the opposite side of the street.

This was where a guy like Monk Purvis would make himself known. Mouse Tyrrell was the daytime bartender. He was a fussy little man who scurried about like his namesake, never seeming to stand still. But Batista knew that he was the one *hombre* in Saragosa who would know if Purvis had made contact. Selling information was a secondary occupation for most guys in his profession. Just like with barbers, people tended to open up to bartenders about all manner of private issues.

He sidled up to the bar and ordered a beer. After sinking half the glass, negotiations began as he posed his question:

'Has anyone been asking about a man called Juan Batista, *señor?*' The rest of the beer then pursued the first half.

Tyrrel scratched his pomaded head, his pinched features twisting in thought.

'Don't rightly know.' He was deliberately prevaricating, hum-ing and hah-ing. 'My memory ain't what it used to be.'

A ten-dollar bill was slapped down on to the counter.

'Will that help bring it back?'

'Errrm . . . could be I do recall something,' came the drawled response as the note disappeared. Tyrrel raised a speculative eyebrow. Twenty bucks was the standard price. Another ten spot then followed the first.

'Yep, now I recollect. A guy did call in two days ago.' Tyrrell's voice sank to a furtive whisper as he continued: 'A real tough customer if'n you ask me. Said he would wait four days only for a Señor Batista in the old Heggerty place. It can be found three miles outside town, heading west on the Van Horn road along a canyon marked by a pile of stones. The information he has concerns the whereabouts of Señor Batista'a long-lost brother.'

The Mexican nodded. 'I will pass on the information. Another glass, barkeep . . . and this one will be on the house, I think.' Mouse Tyrrell showed no sign of dissent — it was all part of the game.

Before he left, Batista asked for a bottle of beer for his partner, who was asleep in the hotel. Take-outs were an accepted practice. Mouse dug under the bar for an empty whiskey bottle, filled it up from the beer tap and sealed the neck with a cork.

His hand, extended to receive the payment, was markedly ignored as the Mexican pulled down his sombrero. Batista's defiant gaze, black as Hades, challenged any objection. It was backed up by the sight of his hand resting on his conspicuous gun butt. The bartender took the hint, opting for the safe response. He had made his dough. And anyway, it wasn't his beer. He only worked here.

Once outside, Batista removed a small phial from his jacket and surreptitiously emptied the contents into the bottle. He swirled the white powder around to dissolve it. While the two so-called partners had been passing through El Paso, Batista had visited the sawbones while Crado was having a shave and haircut. He had deliberately kept the visit secret. For what he had purchased was a strong sleeping draught. A wily smirk crossed the bleak landscape of his face.

A nascent resentment at having to part with half of his father's hard-won loot to a gringo had festered and grown. It had been urged on by his treatment at the hands of the bounty hunter in Safford. Such an experience was impossible to forgive or forget. Every time he thought about that dire episode, shivers rippled through his body, a cold sweat bubbling out on his forehead.

To be sure, he had come to like the bounty hunter, even admire him. But family loyalty came first. As the last of the line, Juan Batista felt it his bounden duty to continue the uprising that his late father had instigated. All of that money would be needed for such a rebellion to succeed.

So Crado Bluestone had to be removed from the field of conflict.

Temporarily of course. Batista had no wish to harm his hoodwinked partner. Just lay him up for a spell. Gain enough time to secure the missing code and disappear. He lifted his eyes to the hotel window behind which his unsuspecting partner was slumbering.

'It is for the best, *mi amigo*,' he muttered under his breath. 'And I will make sure Monk Purvis pays the price for defiling both our lives.'

Back up in their room, Crado was just coming round. He stretched the stiffness from his lean frame.

'I sure feel better for that,' he mumbled.

'Here is some beer I have brought for you,' Batista said with a straight face.

'Cold and straight from the barrel.' He handed over the toxic mixture.

Crado's eyes lit up. 'Just what the doctor ordered.' A rather unfortunate choice of words under the circumstances. 'My mouth feels like the inside of a buffalo skinner's glove.' He wasted no time in grabbing the bottle, flipping off the cork and tipping the contents down his parched throat. He uttered a deep sigh of contentment. He lay back, resting his head on a raised pillow. The remains of the liquor soon disappeared.

'Gee, that was like nectar to the gods. Reckon I ain't never tasted any better.'

The cheerful grin on Batista's face gave nothing away. Nor did the blithe suggestion that followed.

'You take it easy and I will tell you what I found out. No need to hurry. Purvis has not arrived yet, according to the local bartender.'

Crado nodded. He felt a bit lightheaded. Must be from drinking on an empty stomach. He lay back on the bed. The room was becoming hazy, his vision blurred.

'Guess I should have drunk that beer a tad slower,' he murmured.

Five minutes later he was out for the count. Batista covered him with the quilt.

'I am sorry for having to do this, amigo.' It was an apology tinged with genuine regret. 'Another time, another life, perhaps we could have made a good partnership. But Mexico's need is far greater than yourn.'

13

The Devil at Dusk

Not wanting to waste any time, or attract any unwelcome attention, El Vengador sneaked out through the back of the hotel. His horse was already tethered there, along with Bluestone's stallion. He mounted his own horse and led the stallion down to the edge of town, where he left it with a stable boy at the livery. It was a magnificent animal but would require too much getting used to. Batista lacked the time available for such a task. It was a pity but could not be helped.

'See that he is well fed,' the Mexican ordered. 'My partner will be along in a couple of days to collect him. Do you have a mount ready for the trail? My horse is also tired and I am in hurry to depart.'

No explanation was given for the exchange. None was requested. A mere stable hand was not about to question a tough-looking jasper like this greaser.

'We have a couple of horses you could look at,' replied the boy, pointing across to the corral. 'Either will suit. Your horse and twenty bucks, OK?'

Batista would have dearly loved to haggle over the charge. But what he had said was true. He was in a hurry. After ambling over to view the pair of mounts, he forced himself to appear undecided before making his choice. Nevertheless, a natural bartering instinct was in play.

'My horse and ten greenbacks for the chestnut.'

The boy sucked in his cheeks. He was a seasoned hand at this game. He had pushed it up to fifteen before a deal was struck. Eager to get going, Batista quickly saddled his fresh mount and tied his gear to the cantle. With a brisk 'Adios' he spurred off in the direction of the abandoned Heggerty place.

Once he reached the canyon a broken signboard pointed the way. Just legible was the inscription that read: Saul Heggerty — Chicken Farmer, 1 m.

Now that he was close to the final showdown Batista needed to work out how he was going to take possession of the all-important cemetery code and overcome Purvis in the encounter.

His main advantage was that of surprise. The varmint would not be expecting a challenge. As far as he was concerned this was a simple missing-person enquiry. Batista would need to profit from his advantage to gain the upper hand and so emerge victorious. Gingerly he entered the confines of the canyon. It immediately became obvious that, whoever Heggerty was, he had long since abandoned the place. The trail was now little more than a deer run. With eyes peeled for any sign of recent occupation the rider remained tense and alert.

Ten minutes later he spotted the rough-hewn cabin up ahead. And there was a horse tethered outside. A twirl of smoke wound from the stovepipe. His quarry had arrived. Purvis must have seen the old signboard and investigated. Finding the shack abandoned, he had evidently judged this to be a good place to, as he supposed, sell his information. The Mexican's face cracked in an anticipatory snarl.

'At long last, *El Vengador* will have his revenge. And you, Señor Purvis, will get your just deserts.'

He dismounted in the cover of a copse of palo verde trees. Having checked the load of his revolver, he moved cautiously towards the cabin. He could detect no movement. All was quiet. But the varmint had to be there. Batista knew that he would need to exercise far more care now that he was operating alone,

Perhaps it would be best to wait in the cover of some rocks until Purvis emerged from the cabin. The gringo would need to feed his horse and draw water from the creek. Satisfied that this was the best option, Batista settled down to await developments. He did not have to wait long. The appearance of the killer was from where he would have least expected.

'Stay right where you are, greaser.' The low yet intimidating command came from behind. Batista's whole body tensed. 'Now shuck those guns and step out into the open where I can see your ugly mush.'

The Mexican froze. He had been totally outfoxed.

'Move it, I said!' The tone was harsh and menacing. 'And get them mitts sky-bound.' A click of the Remington Rider to full cock emphasized the fact that the guy meant business.

Batista was given no choice but to obey. It was too late now to regret his shameful tactics in incapacitating his partner.

Monk Purvis was by nature a suspicious dude. When he read the missing person notice in the *West Texas Echo* his devious mind took little time in working out the true nature of the enquiry. This greaser Juan Batista wanted the missing half of the cemetery code. If by some chance, it did turn out to be a genuine desire for family information, he could easily concoct a story to satisfy the guy. It would earn him a few bucks for his trouble.

But deep within his being, Purvis knew the score. Here was his chance to secure that code and go dig up the loot. A vision of a life of ease floated glittering before his rapacious gaze as he made tracks for Saragosa.

As the sun disappeared over the scalloped rim of the canyon, an owl hooted. Shadows were settling over the harsh terrain. Was it an omen of doom? Batista was given no time to contemplate his destiny.

'Now hand over that missing code, and I'll be on my way,' Purvis snarled. 'Otherwise it's goodbye world. Ain't nobody comes up here any more. So I have plenty of time to persuade you that it's the right thing to do.'

'Never, never!' hollered the Mexican. 'You kill my father first, then my brother to get your filthy hands on that code. I will die before surrendering other half.' His back stiffened. The unyielding stance challenged Purvis to do his worst.

The killer smiled. Now he knew for certain that his supposition had been correct. He spat out a rancid growl.

'If'n you don't play ball, it's gonna be a mighty painful way to end your days, Juan.'

Not waiting for a reply he pulled the trigger of the large gun. A heavy bullet smashed into Batista's kneecap. He screamed and fell to the ground clutching at the shattered joint.

'And that's only the start.' Bending low, Purvis dragged out a ten-inch Bowie knife from its sheath in his boot. 'This beauty can do a heap of damage to soft flesh.' Purposefully, a manic grin swathing his brutish visage, he closed the gap.

Batista's eyes widened in terror as the

blade swung down. His left ear became a mangled rag of bloody, torn skin. But the torture had only just begun. The blade-wielder knew his craft. Yet still the stubborn Mexican held out.

Monk Purvis knew from previous encounters with obstinate critters that it was only a matter of time before pain and suffering took their toll. It was no different for Juan Batista. Machismo inherent in every *hombre Mejicano* can only hold out for so long under such brutal chastisement.

★ ★ ★

Crado woke up with a splitting headache. One bottle of beer? He knew that he'd only had the one. Had it been that strong? The sun was shining through the open window. Outside he could hear the general hubbub of a town going about its regular business. How long had he been asleep? He leaned up on one elbow. Another jolt of pain shot through his head. Where had Juan got to?

After another half-hour he felt slightly better. Struggling off the bed, still fully clothed, he splashed some cold water into a bowl and doused his head. The shock soon brought him round to a more lucid frame of mind. He dried off, then slapped his hat on and stepped gingerly out of the room. His head was still woozy and he felt unsteady on his feet. A good breakfast would soon sort him out. Then he needed to find Juan. What was the guy doing? In the foyer of the hotel Crado spoke to the clerk on duty.

'What day is it, buddy?' he asked in all innocence.

The man gave him a sideways glance. 'Thursday, sir,' he replied.

'Thursday? Where in tarnation did Wednesday go?'

He was totally dumbfounded. The clerk gave the customer a wary look as if his sanity was a tad unhinged. Crado shook the mush from his head. He didn't wait for a reply, instead tumbling out on to the street. Two days gone and he had known nothing about it. Something was wrong here, and it all came down to that bottle of beer.

Slowly but surely the thought processes inside his head were beginning to cohere. Juan Batista had slipped him a Mickey Finn. There could be only one reason for that. He wanted that code for himself.

Crado blurted out a vivid expletive that caused two ladies hurrying by to give him a wide berth.

'You rotten treacherous skunk!' he growled out, heading straight for the saloon. That was the place to find out if Purvis had arrived yet.

Moss Tyrrell was polishing the bar top. 'What'll it be, stranger?'

'Information, that's all,' Crado snapped.

Tyrrell settled into his dealer's mode of behaviour. 'So what is it you wish to know?' The unctuous smile did nothing to endear him to the questioner.

'Has a greaser been in here asking after some dude called Purvis?'

'Waaaaaaaal noooooow!' drawled the barman stroking one of his chins. 'I ain't rightly sure about that.'

Crado's eyes narrowed to thin slits. He was good and mad, and no smarmy bar weasel was going to fob him off. Without any warning he leaned over and grabbed Tyrrell by the shirt front, dragging him halfway across the shiny counter.

'Now listen up, dog's breath. I asked you a question.' The statement was stacked mountain high with ugly hints of what would follow should the guy stall any longer. 'Answer it and you get to live another day.'

The barman quickly blurted out the required reply. Crado released him with a brief apology before leaving the saloon. Now he needed to find his horse. More time was wasted asking around, a task that led him down to the livery stable where he spotted Dusky in the corral. He looked to be in good condition.

'That your horse, mister?' The enquiry came from a young lad who was forking hay into a pile. 'He sure is one fine mount. The guy who left him here paid me up front for his keep.'

'Was he a greaser?'

The boy nodded. 'He wore the biggest sombrero I ever did see this side of the border. And he was in a darned hurry too.'

'That's Batista all right.' Crado was fuming. 'Which way did he go?'

The boy pointed to the east. 'Down the Van Horn road.'

Crado threw the kid a silver dollar for his help and saddled up. He was soon on the trail chewing on a burrito obtained from the local cafe. Moss Tyrrell had passed on the same information he had given Batista. Crado gave Dusky his head and they ate up the three miles to the canyon turn-off in double-quick time. There was little doubt that whomsoever had triumphed in the confrontation was now on their way south. That said, Crado was forced to rein the stallion in along the hazardous canyon bottom.

What he found outside Heggarty's old cabin was a nauseating shock to the system. Batista's bloodstained corpse was barely recognizable. Crado's stomach lurched uncontrollably, discharging the contents on to the sandy ground. The poor guy was still breathing. But his days were clearly numbered.

'Why in blue blazes did you have to be so greedy?' he ranted at the clump of human detritus. 'There's sure to be enough in that grave for the both of us. Two guys working together could have handled the skunk. Now once again, Monk Purvis has the upper hand.'

Batista passed away moments later. Crado left the body for the scavengers to feast on. It looked like they had already begun. With Purvis two days ahead, no time for a burial of the remains could be afforded. He mounted up and thankfully swung away from the grisly scene.

'It's up to you, boy,' he murmured

into the twitching ears. Dusky would now have to offer proof that an arab stallion's staying power was three times that of a regular horse

14

Hangman's Reach

Three days later the furious pursuer reached Fort Hancock on the banks of the Rio Grande. At this point the river narrowed sufficiently for a ferry to operate. It was a busy crossing point, with all manner of goods and people making use of the facility to enter the Mexican province of Chihuahua. Sentries posted on the American side maintained a close watch on all those wishing to make the crossing.

The army's prime duty was to ensure that no undesirables entered the United States. There existed numerous other places where a clandestine crossing could be made, but the military presence at Fort Hancock had been established to send a clear message to the Mexican government that the border separating their two countries was not to be violated.

To avoid any delay Crado made a point of wearing his US deputy marshal's badge to provide him with the legal authority to cross. Not that he expected any trouble. Crossing into Mexico was not the problem. Most checks were made on those coming in the opposite direction, particularly on the wagons.

He still had to register with the local sheriff, though. Perhaps he could have made the crossing downriver in secret, but this was his first visit to Mexico and he had no wish to lose his way amidst the untamed wilderness that stretched away south of the Big Muddy.

'How did you come to be given this badge, Mr Bluestone?' Sheriff Ryker Chisum asked suspiciously. 'That sort of authority is only handed out by the Rangers under special circumstances.'

Crado went on to briefly outline his meeting with Jack Banner. He explained how the Chief Ranger had given him the authority to hunt down the man who had tried to hang him after stealing his cattle.

Chisum's manner changed as soon as he heard the name of the legendary Texas Ranger.

'Me and Jack rode together for a spell back in '72 before I came down here. If'n he gave you this, it's for a good cause.'

'Monk Purvis also killed another ranger called Ezra Quinn,' Crado went on. 'I'm on his trail now. The skunk tortured and killed a friend of mine near Saragosa only three days ago. He managed to tell me Purvis was headed this way before he croaked. So I now have a whole bagful of reasons to bring the rat in . . . dead or alive!'

'You have my sympathies, Crado,' the lawman told him. 'Anything I can do to help, just say the word. I knew Ezra well. He was a good man.'

'All I need are the directions to reach a place called Camposanto. That's where Purvis is heading.'

The sheriff frowned. A sceptical expression clouded the lawman's gnarled features.

'The only thing at Composanto is a large cemetery. What in blue blazes could the varmint want there?'

Crado contrived to put a look of equal puzzlement upon his own countenance. The last thing he intended was to reveal the additional reason for chasing down the outlaw.

'Do you know how to reach this place?'

The main trail avoided broken country that lay immediately to the south. But there was a quicker way, straight across the desert.

'Head south-west across the salt flats until you hit a prominent butte called St Xavier's Spine. You can't miss it. From there turn due east. Composanto is another two days' ride on the edge of the wilderness.' The starman scratched his balding pate. 'Mighty strange destination for an outlaw and killer,' he mused. 'Mighty strange.'

To distract Chisum from any unwelcome conclusions he might seek to draw, Crado brought the conversation round to more immediate practical matters.

'I ain't eaten a decent meal for a week, Sheriff. Can you recommend a good hash house?'

The sheriff rubbed his abdomen. Food was one of his favourite topics of conversation.

'You won't do better than Milly Dink's Western Diner. Tell her I sent you. Best steaks this side of the Canadian border.' He kissed his fingers. '*Magnifico*.'

Ryker Chisum sure wasn't wrong there, as Crado was able to testify when he rode out of Fort Hancock and on to the ferry. He encountered no problems when he presented the signed pass from the sheriff to the guard on duty at the landing stage.

* * *

Navigation across the sterile white of the salt flats was accomplished by means of the sun. St. Xavier's Spine was a near perfect copy of a church steeple. It was named after the highly respected missionary who had allegedly paused here to give thanks to the Lord for safe deliverance from the bleak wasteland he had just crossed.

Five days later Crado passed out of the desert into a more benign landscape. The harsh sculpture of broken rock and sandy wasteland slowly surrendered its grip. Orange and dun brown gave way to dull greens with the odd splash of yellow. More trees were able to flourish where he encountered the first creek. A thin, muddy affair, it was still water. His horse drank deeply.

Another day passed before he sighted a cluster of desiccated palo verde interspersed with Joshua trees. They formed a macabre guard of honour encircling the bone yard wherein lay the secret of the Batista horde.

Crado circled around the whole place, making a point of keeping below the crest to avoid observation by any visitors. Juan Batista had not been exaggerating. Camposanto cemetery was huge. It was situated in a depression akin to a giant bowl. Only when he had reached the far side did Crado espy a lone horse tied to the main access gate. Nobody else was in sight.

Could this mean Monk Purvis was here? After all this time, would vengeance be within his grasp? His searching finger pawed at the rough scar encircling his neck. The blood inside his head was pounding. The wronged man-hunter's whole being burned with the desire to race down there and call him out.

Then he remembered his own advice. Breathe deep, adopt a cool, detached approach if'n you wanted to come out of this fracas a winner. It might not even be Purvis down there. Obeying his own diktat, Crado nudged the black stallion down the slope.

As he drew near, his heart skipped a beat. Was that his saddle on the other horse? Another squinted look confirmed his suspicion. No doubt about it. Even seen from a distance of one hundred yards, there could only ever be one like that. Custom-made to his own specifications, it had been a prized possession. Then that dry-gulcher had come along and ruined his life.

Well, he was gonna pay a heavy price now that the final showdown was nigh.

A movement somewhere in the heart of the graveyard caught Crado's attention. His narrowed stare picked out a lone visitor, digging beside a tombstone. The grave was thrown into shade by one of the few cottonwoods dotted about the cemetery. All of the critter's attention was focused on the task of excavating what was buried in the hard ground.

The watcher smiled to himself. He tethered the black out of sight. His long legs made easy work of the boundary fence. Tentatively Crado cat-footed over the stony ground to where Purvis was labouring with a feverish intensity.

There he paused, hidden from view behind a large stone carving of the Madonna, gathering himself for the final showdown.

A light breeze disturbed the dried leaves of the cottonwood. Flakes of white drifted down on to the digger's bare tonsured head. It was Purvis all right. The killer idly brushed the flakes away, completely unaware of the danger immediately to his rear.

The name on the nearby gravestone brought a knowing curl to Crado's lip: Esteban Batista, husband of Maria and father to Hernando, 1810-1858. So the old guy had buried the money in the family plot. It made perfect sense.

Gun gripped firmly in his right hand, Crado rose and stepped out into the open. Another pace and his shadow fell across the deepening trench. Purvis froze, suddenly realizing that he was not alone. His swung his head to his left. A fear-stricken jolt of alarm registered on the skunk's bearded face.

'Don't stop on my account, Monk.'

The chilling command cut through the still air. 'Just keep on digging until you find it.'

Purvis didn't move. His brain was struggling to recall where he had heard that voice before. In the meantime he would play for time.

'Don't know what you mean, mister. I'm just a simple guy preparing this grave for a burial,' he responded, quickly regaining his equanimity. 'Have we met before?' Clearly they had, as this jasper knew his name.

'Let me remind you,' snarled Crado. 'Remember the Brazos five years back when you and your buddies strung me up and then stole my cattle? You left me to croak out my life by that creek, figuring I'd be buzzard bait.'

The owlhooter's face blanched. He turned to look at this sudden apparition from the past.

'Y-you! But it can't be.' Was he looking at a ghost, a figment of his imagination? 'You couldn't have survived that . . . '

A maniacal laugh echoed across the place of death. 'But I did, as you can plainly see, thanks to the lucky arrival of a Texas Ranger. And now here I am, alive and well, just itching to give you a similar send-off.'

Purvis was too stunned to do anything. His whole body felt like it was trapped in a seizure. One minute he had been contemplating a life of unbridled ease and luxury, now extinction stared him in the face. He tried shaking the turgid morass from inside his head. This couldn't be happening. But it was. And he needed to do something about it, and fast.

'Now get that shovel moving, you sonofabitch.' Crado's entire being was eaten up with the need for revenge, the final reckoning for a wrong which had been with him for too long. 'I'm getting mighty impatient to get my hands on that dough,' he rasped. 'Then you'll enjoy a taste of your own medicine. But this time, there won't be no cure. Doctor Death will be hauling back on the rope.'

He laughed out loud at the gallows humour.

The bounty hunter's euphoria at running his prey to earth had, however, made him careless. One of the first precepts in the man-hunting game was to neutralize your opponent. Purvis was still armed. His hand was even now sliding down to grasp the butt of his trusty Remington. His body twisted as the gun cleared leather and rose. A shot rang out.

In the nick of time Crado realized his error. His habitual caution had been distracted by avarice and the desire for wrath. The two deadly sins had blinded him.

He ducked down. The bullet struck the statue. Fragments of stone flew off. Before the wily outlaw could get off a second shot, Crado's own revolver barked twice. One of the bullets lifted the would-be killer's hat. The other smashed into the gun in Purvis's hand. It was a perfect shot. Purvis suffered no physical injury other than a numbed arm as the Remington was wrenched from his grasp. He cried out, clutching at his aching wrist.

Crado gave him no further chance to play the foxy card. He jumped forward and slammed the barrel of his own gun down on Purvis's head. The killer slumped over, pole-axed.

Crado wasted no time. He dragged the unconscious man out of the hole and tied him up with his own belt and suspenders. Then he went off and brought the guy's horse back to the grave.

He commandeered the shovel and continued with the excavation. Five minutes later the shovel struck something hard. His eyes glazed over. Was this the hidden loot that Juan Batista was so adamant his father had buried here all those years ago? It had to be. His hands busily scrabbled away the sand to reveal a strongbox. His breath caught in his throat. Quickly he man-handled the heavy stash up to the surface.

The lock was rusted solid with age and the elements. A well-placed bullet smashed it to bits. Hardly daring to breathe, he slowly opened the lid. His probing eyes bulged like duck eggs at what he found inside. He rubbed his peepers, unable to believe what they revealed.

Nothing. Not even a measly wooden nickel. The box was empty, apart from a grubby piece of paper. He read the brief missive, his mouth hanging askew. Then he burst out laughing. A reflexive response to the shock. He slapped his thighs as tears rolled down his stubbled cheeks. All this way, all that planning, to find that the loot had already been dug up. Was that not the ultimate joke? Or should he rather be crying with rage?

Again he read the message. *The money you hoped to find in this grave has been put to a worthier cause. It is now in the hands of the People's Freedom Movement and will be spent on arms to further the revolution.* There was no signature. Only the date: 23 May, 1860. That was sixteen years ago.

Crado was too stunned, too mesmerized to react. It was a sound on the tethered horse that jerked him back to reality and made him look up.

Purvis had been dumped astride the saddle, hands tied behind his back. A noose was tied around his thick neck. It was secured to an overhanging branch of the cottonwood. The critter had only just regained consciousness. Not yet aware of his dire predicament, Purvis mumbled, 'What's so darned funny?'

Another burst of frenzied jocularity rang out across the graveyard. Birds lifted from their perches dismayed by this unfamiliar cackling. A desert rat poked its head from a hole beneath an adjacent tombstone.

'All this effort and there ain't no reward at the end of it.' Crado's remark was heavy with sarcasm. There was in truth no humorous side to the unexpected discovery. He held the box up for the prisoner to see. 'It's empty, not a single bean left for my trouble.'

Purvis now suddenly found himself the guest of honour at his own hanging. He burbled, mouthing protestations about his bleak situation

'What's going on? You can't hang me. It ain't legal.'

That piece of bent wisdom was certainly worth another howl of laughter.

'The only thing a skunk like you knows about the law is how to break it,' scoffed Crado. 'In any case, I ain't gonna hang you.' A mirthless smirk followed. 'Your cayuse will do the job for me.'

He then left the gabbling captive and went to fill up a bucket with water from a well near the entrance to the cemetery. It had been dug especially for relatives of the dearly departed who wished to leave flowers on the graves. Water from it was now going to serve as an inducement to the killer's horse when he became thirsty.

He placed the bucket some six feet

away from the standing animal.

'Soon or later, this old mustang is gonna feel the need to slake his thirst. Get my drift, Monk? You can blame him for making you take the hangman's reach. It ain't my doing.'

Crado turned to walk away.

'Hey, fella,' Purvis beseeched. Desperation was scrawled across his visage. 'Don't do this to me. It ain't . . . American. That was a mistake on the Brazos. I always intended to come back. It was the other guys who forced my hand.'

The bounty hunter paused. He swung around. A dark glower of hatred had replaced the manic grin.

'That kind of excuse don't even merit a reply,' he spat back. 'See you around in the next life, sucker.'

He had only got as far as the well when he spotted a rider approaching. He cursed the bad timing. Straining his eye, he picked out a high-crowned hat. The sun was glinting off a metal badge pinned to the rider's leather vest. Then the nickel dropped. It was Jack Banner.

What in the name of Old Nick was he doing in Chihuahua? The rider drew up facing his old associate.

'You ain't leaving him there are you, Crado? Action like that goes against everything I expected when I gave you that US marshal's badge. I've come down here to take Purvis back to stand trial in Austin. He'll get a fair hearing and a judge will pronounce sentence if'n he's found guilty. You ain't in the business of dealing out vigilante law.'

'Goldarn it, Jack!' Crado exclaimed in frustration. 'You know what the skunk did. He deserves to sweat buckets before taking the reach. Especially when there was no darned loot buried in that grave.'

Banner suppressed a smile at that disclosure. 'What you're doing ain't right,' he insisted. 'I expected more from you. Any man who wears the badge should live up to the high ideals of the service.'

'I tried, believe me,' Crado countered. 'But it didn't suit my temperament. Guess

I ain't cut out to be a lawman.' He went on to briefly explain the circumstances that had brought him to the Camposanto cemetery and the showdown with Monk Purvis. The Texas Ranger listened without interruption. It was a fascinating story. When he'd finished, Crado's face creased into a puzzled frown.

'How did you know to come down here anyway?'

'I heard tell you and some greaser had caused a fracas in Tucson. There was a dodger out on you. Since that day on the Brazos I've been following your career.' He rolled a smoke and threw the makings down to the other man. They both enjoyed the moment before Banner resumed: 'And it's been a mighty interesting revelation. You turning bounty hunter I could just about stomach. But what I couldn't believe was that the guy whose neck I'd saved was a two-bit gunslinger. So I made it my business to find out the truth.'

'That shooting of Rowdy Slag Bassett was all a big — '

243

'Don't worry, you're in the clear,' Banner interjected with a smile. 'I tracked you to Silver City where that singer in the Golden Nugget spoke up for you. She sure seemed mighty keen to clear your name. Some'n between you two?' He lifted his eyes, hoping for a response. Crado's flushed cheeks and bashful shrug gave him the answer.

Banner smiled. 'I figured that must be it.' Then he went on, 'Seems like the local tinstar was overstepping his authority in Tucson.'

'You ain't wrong there, buddy,' rasped Crado.

Banner leaned over the neck of his horse. His face hardened into a pugnacious challenge as he nodded towards the sorry spectacle beneath the cottonwood.

'Just like you are doing over yonder. You disappoint me, Crado. I gave you that badge to bring the jasper in, not behave like a one-man punishment squad.'

To his credit, Crado Bluestone was

suitably crestfallen, deflated. Banner had hit a raw nerve of conscience. He felt bad now at having abused the trust this stolid defender of law and order had placed in him.

'The Mexican authorities granted permission for me to come down here and take him back. But I can't do it alone.' Banner held the bounty hunter's awkward gaze. The unspoken offer of redemption was there. 'If'n you're with me on this, I'm gonna need a quick answer. That cayuse over there is getting a mite frisky.'

At that moment Purvis called out. 'Hey mister, you ain't gonna let this guy hang an innocent man, are you?'

A look of disbelief on Crado's face was matched by one on Banner's, both seeming to say, silently: *This guy needs an official court ruling to put him straight*.

'Guess I can make a detour with you before I head back to Silver City,' Crado said.

'Glad to hear it. And maybe on the

way to Austin, I can persuade you to take up the vacant post of sheriff in Tucson.' The Texas Ranger paused to allow the import of his suggestion to take root. 'Iron Bart Maston has been encouraged to resign on account of actions unbecoming to the spirit of law enforcement. His term of office ends next month. I've persuaded the town council to keep the vacancy open.'

Another squeal from the panic-stricken captive drew the two *compadres* across the graveyard towards him. But they were in no hurry to relieve the pressure on Monk Purvis's neck from the Hangman's Reach.

We do hope that you have enjoyed reading this large print book.

Did you know that all of our titles are available for purchase?

We publish a wide range of high quality large print books including:
**Romances, Mysteries, Classics
General Fiction
Non Fiction and Westerns**

Special interest titles available in large print are:
**The Little Oxford Dictionary
Music Book, Song Book
Hymn Book, Service Book**

Also available from us courtesy of Oxford University Press:
**Young Readers' Dictionary
(large print edition)
Young Readers' Thesaurus
(large print edition)**

For further information or a free brochure, please contact us at:
**Ulverscroft Large Print Books Ltd.,
The Green, Bradgate Road, Anstey,
Leicester, LE7 7FU, England.
Tel:** (00 44) **0116 236 4325
Fax:** (00 44) **0116 234 0205**

*Other titles in the
Linford Western Library:*

RED CANYON RED

Billy Hall

Some call her Red Kenyon the Red Canyon hellcat — and the young woman with an unmanageable tangle of red hair has proved herself the equal of most men on more than one occasion. But Red is only beginning to realize her mistake in trying to go after the stolen heifers alone. Far from any possibility of rescue, Leif Mortenson leers at the disarmed and helpless nemesis who has twice thwarted him. As panic and despair wash over her, Red knows she has the toughest fight of her life ahead . . .

SALOON

Owen G. Irons

Diane Kingsley, part-owner of the Cock's Crow Saloon, has made one too many enemies, and finally they've seen to it that she was thrown aboard a westbound train and sent out alone into the desert. Well . . . not quite alone, for, when she arrives, she finds that she has been riding with Walt Cassidy, who has also been run out of Sand Hill, for shooting the man who killed his horse. Walt is desperate — and intrigued by Diane's plan to build a saloon in an empty land . . .

GUNS OF SANTA CARMELITA

Hugh Martin

When former deputy town marshal Frank Calland helps out another saddle-tramp whom he finds stranded without food or water in the Arizona desert, he ends up being pursued by an angry posse — but this is only the beginning of his problems. He finds himself donning the lawman's star once more, this time as deputy to Marshal Bill Riggs, who seems to be hiding a dark secret from his past. Calland is thrown into the deep end, and must take responsibility when a band of ruthless outlaws arrives, blood-thirsty for revenge . . .